CASE FILES FROM THE NIG

THE MUMMY'S VENGEANCE

DAVID ALYN GORDON

For my love Gwyneth
and
All the Creative Geniuses in the Literary and Cinematic
World that Influenced My Imagination

Acknowledgements

I would like to thank the following people for making this work and series a reality:

My wife Dr. Gwyneth Gordon for her endless support through the years.

My family and friends for their encouragement.

My students, teachers, and staff at Grand Canyon College Preparatory Academy.

Miblart for the cover art.

Ms Tonia Designs for the formatting.

Natalie Bavar for providing valuable feedback by both beta reading and line editing.

Nicki Synder for beta reading and providing valuable feedback.

Chapter One

1317 B.C.E.
Memphis, the Capital of Lower Egypt

The High Priest Sennefer rallied his priests to gather all their possessions at their temple for the Sun God, Aten. The forces of the old order, led by General Nakhtmin, were fast-approaching to lay siege and purge all remnants of the religion the Pharaoh Akhenaten had founded. The new Pharaoh, Horemheb, had more forcefully continued the work of his predecessors, Tutankhamun and Ay, in literally tearing down all the remaining signs of Atenism, including the priests who preached the monotheistic faith and monuments to Akhenaten.

Sennefer hoped that he and a few of his priests might be able to escape to a remote part of Egypt and continue practicing their faith, waiting for the day when Atenism would gain prominence again.

One of the priests, Ramose, rushed over to Sennefer and handed him a small, oval-shaped crystal. "Holiness, the Eye of Aten."

"Thank you, Ramose," Sennefer said, taking the crystal with both hands. "Now go... Meet us at the agreed destination."

"Aten is great of majesty and in my heart," Ramose replied and started to run off.

Unfortunately, when he turned, he ran directly into the tall and dark-haired General Nakhtmin. The leader smiled and thrust his short sword into Ramose's abdomen.

Ramose gasped and fell to the ground, clutching his stomach.

Sennefer rushed over and cradled his head. "Aten be with you in the next life, Ramose."

"He is in my heart," Ramose said with his last breath, eyes closing.

"There is no escape for you and your priests today, heretic," Nakhtmin said, raising his bloody sword. "Your turn, now." He drove the weapon into Sennefer's torso.

The priest, in agony, slumped over Ramose. He felt life leaving him, but with his remaining energy, he pulled himself up to look at the General, gasping as Nakhtmin's sword tore further into his body. He held up the Eye of Aten and furiously stared at Nakhtmin. "I look forward to my journey to the next life. But that journey is not for you. You are the desecrator and the true heretic, and I, a priest of Aten, curse you to wander this world for all eternity. The next life will be barred to you until you harness the power of the eye and speak the sacred words of Aten."

"Time for you to go to the next life," Nakhtmin said, pulling the sword out of Sennefer and raising it over his shoulder.

Abram, working as a mercenary, entered the temple as Nakhtmin struck the killing blow.

Thousands of years, he thought, *and humanity is still as brutal as ever.* "Was it necessary to kill them in their own temple?"

"Just following the Pharoah's orders," Nakhtmin said, wiping his sword on Sennefer's robes. "See to the disposal of these heretics. These traitors are not to be mummified and will not receive purification rites. Bury them in unmarked graves."

"Yes, General."

"The old fool cursed me to immortality." Nakhtmin scoffed. "Like that's supposed to be a punishment. At least I know what this life is like."

Abram smiled, thinking, *At least I'll have someone else to talk to in about 100 years if this curse is real.*

Two of Abram's soldiers entered the temple to request new orders.

Abram whispered, "Take the high priest to the house of Thutmose. We may not be able to do the full mummification process, but we can, at the very least, bandage him and give him some semblance of respect."

CHAPTER TWO

August 22, 1920
Royal Oak, Michigan

I ndustrialist and robber baron Malcom Thorne, who looked like a blend of J. P. Morgan and John Rockefeller, ordered his attorney and trusted confidant, Blake Cartwright, to do a background check on Reverend John Sullivan.

Cartwright dug up some clippings in the Hearst Press about this small-town religious figure who whipped his flock into a frenzy, denouncing the League of Nations, Woodrow Wilson's retreat from isolationism, Black migration to the North, Jewish bankers, red Communists, socialists, unionists, and anarchists.

Now this *is a man who thinks like me,* Thorne thought to himself, skimming through the information Cartwright had presented.

On this Sunday, August 22, 1920, Thorne and Cartwright attended the sermon of Reverend John Sullivan for the first time. Thorne was mesmerized by the oratory skills and charismatic presence of the tall, balding, religious firebrand from Royal

Oak, Michigan.

"It is time, my children, to do what Senator Harding suggests and return to normalcy. And what is normalcy?" Sullivan paused to gaze at his flock. "Normalcy is staying out of the League of Nations. Normalcy is going back to what life was like before getting involved in the European war." His speech took up a rhythmic quality, moving from item to item with increasing energy. "Normalcy is telling the black man to go back south where he belongs, so he doesn't take our jobs away. Normalcy is sending all non-white immigrants back to Italy and Russia with the other reds before they destroy this country from within. Normalcy is about us having the lives we all deserve without outsiders coming in to ruin it. Normalcy is not letting anyone dictate how we live, especially not Zionist rats, the pope, atheists like Lenin and Trotsky, and the king of England!"

Thorne was impressed that the devoted crowd was completely in sync with Sullivan. They cheered, fell silent, and applauded as though they'd received a script.

After the sermon was over, and the congregation dispersed, Thorne sent Cartwright to request a meeting with Sullivan.

Sullivan, recognizing the name and importance of Malcom Thorne, jumped at the chance to connect with one of America's richest. He practically ran to clasp his hands. "It is a pleasure to meet you, Mr. Thorne."

"Likewise, Reverend. I admire what you have to say and how you inspire the people in your flock. You have a gift."

"Thank you," Sullivan replied. "I try. We are at such a critical juncture in our history."

"I agree," Thorne said. "I understand you... inherited this assignment last year."

"My predecessor, Reverend Lee, passed away after 60 years of serving the Lord," Sullivan said, nodding gravely. "I was fortunate to be his assistant when he passed on. The congregation board supported my elevation."

"Timing is key to personal opportunity," Thorne said, "And I'd like to offer you an opportunity to speak from a bigger platform and play a role in shaping how our nation moves forward. I am, of course, prepared to back my words with money." Thorne smiled. "How would you like a bigger microphone to spread your message?"

Sullivan was taken aback. "What do you mean?"

"How would you like to take your message across the nation?"

"It would be a great honor if our holy crusade could reach the American people as a whole, and we could shape the nation's soul to His word."

"Of course. Care to join me at my hotel for dinner?"

"It would be my pleasure."

"Excellent. My attorney, Mr. Cartwright, will give you my hotel information," Thorne said, turning away. "Before I forget," he paused and turned back. "I understand you have an interest in ancient civilizations and biblical archeology."

Sullivan nodded. "With the British now seizing Palestine from the heathen Turk, it is a dream I have to go to that region and explore the origins of the Biblical word."

"Very good," Thorne said. "We must also discuss this shared interest tonight."

After saying goodbye to Thorne and Cartwright, Sullivan smiled and went back to his study in the church. It was the same study Reverend Lee had used during the last twenty years of his service. Sullivan sat and thought back to the last time he met with Reverend Lee.

The old man had told Sullivan that he had no intention of retiring, as the community still needed him. Not only that, but he also planned on speaking to the congregation board about reassigning Sullivan because his message to the flock was exclusionary and prejudiced.

The old man did not understand I was on a mission from the Lord to help this country remain The City on the Hill. Sullivan shook his head. *I did what I had to do.* On a quiet afternoon, he'd put rat poison in Lee's tea and watched the old man drink it. *Waste not, want not.* He sat in his small office across the hall and waited for the poison to take effect. It took about half an hour, and Lee, in what looked like a heart attack, fell face down on his desk.

Sullivan smiled to himself. *The Lord helps those who help themselves.*

He waited another half hour before he "discovered" Reverend Lee, so all attempts at resuscitation would be a lost cause. After the funeral, it didn't take much to convince the congregation board to give him the leadership of the church. He'd been building relationships with them since he was hired as Lee's assistant.

Now that Thorne had taken notice of him and made such a generous offer, it was time for good things to come to him.

CHAPTER THREE

F ear was in the hearts of many of the diggers at the Memphis Valley Site 300 miles outside Ancient Memphis. The news of Lord Carnarvon's passing the night before sparked anxiety that The Pharaoh's Curse was alive and well and would descend upon the desecrators of the royal tombs in the Valley of the Kings.

Lead archeologist and project supervisor Trevor Grantham, a 35-year-old, Oxford-educated Anglo-Egyptian, met with his labor foremen and stressed that it was important to convince the workers that no curse from Pharaoh Tutankhamun killed Carnarvon. It was an infection caused by shaving off a mosquito bite. They had nothing to worry about. The foremen agreed to speak with the men but said some would be harder to convince.

"Do the best you can and let me know if there are any groups or individuals I need to speak to directly."

"Yes, effendi," one of the foremen said.

Grantham went back to his tent and was greeted by an armed guard standing outside and his expedition sponsor sitting in his chair. American industrialist and amateur Egyptologist, Malcom Thorne, was lounging and sipping lemonade.

"You're too gentle with these superstitious diggers, Grantham. If they complain or wallow in fear, just let them go and find some more. There are plenty of inexpensive laborers to pick from."

"I'd rather deal with the people I know," Grantham replied, pouring some lemonade for himself. "It's better to demonstrate you understand their beliefs and concerns. You get more out of them that way."

Thorne made a sour face. "You sound like my socialist-loving children. What is this world coming to?"

"God knows," Grantham said, not wanting to annoy his snobby, plutocratic patron. "Still, it does make one pause."

"What?"

"Carnarvon's death."

"Oh, come on," Thorne said, straightening in his seat. "The idiot didn't know how to take care of himself, and he got an infection. If there was a mummy's curse, you would think their project leader would have croaked first because he entered Tut's tomb first."

Grantham smiled. "I suppose. By the way, where is your partner, Sullivan?"

"He's looking at a couple of potential excavation sites in Palestine. I'll let you know what he finds, if anything. Now let's get a progress report. When do you think we'll find the burial site?"

"One or two days at the earliest. A week at the most."

"Good," Thorne said, nodding. "We have to beat that scoundrel Spade."

"We haven't had any interference from him since we received the permits."

"Let's keep it that way," Thorne replied.

One of the foremen, Mosiah, burst into the tent, slightly out of breath. "Effendi, we have a problem."

"Is it the diggers, Mosiah?" Grantham asked, putting down his lemonade.

"No, effendi. Mehemet Andoheb is here."

Grantham's facial expression shifted from concern to frustration. "It's not even lunch time, and this day seems like it will go on forever."

"Who is Meh… who's this guy?" Thorne asked.

"A troublemaker," Grantham replied, pausing in the opening of the tent. "He wreaks havoc at archeological digs across the country."

"He could be an agent of Spade. Have some of our guards take care of him."

"He's no agent of Spade. I'll try and deal with him first before we sic the dogs on him. Take me to him, Mosiah."

"I'll come with you," Thorne said.

Grantham's face now grew horrified at the prospect of Thorne throwing his bigoted, elitist weight around the dig site. "No, sir. He's not worth your valuable time. I can handle it."

Thorne nodded. "If you think that's best."

"I do. Come on, Mosiah."

Grantham noticed that several of the diggers who'd been expressing their fears to the foremen had gathered around Mehemet Andohenb, his mind jumping to all the delays this rabble-rouser could cause.

"Mehemet," Grantham said, offering his hand. "How can I help you?"

"You heard about Lord Carnarvon's passing, Grantham?" Andoheb said, taking Grantham's hand.

"Of course. What of it?"

"It is a sign from the Gods that you and the other expeditions must stop desecrating the resting places of our dead."

"Come on, Mehemet. You were educated at Cambridge. You don't believe in these curses any more than I do."

"And you have Egyptian ancestors like I do," Andoheb said, eyes flashing. "Just because I was educated by the imperialists does not mean I have abandoned my beliefs. I beg you, Grantham. Leave this site before your team suffers the vengeance of the ancient Egyptian gods."

"We will not be scared by this superstitious dribble," Grantham said, hoping he could speak courage into his men. "I think you should leave. My American patron is not as understanding as I am. The next time you show yourself, he'll sic the armed guards on you."

"Very well. You've been warned." Anodheb shook his head. "Whatever happens is on you and your American Patron."

As Andoheb left the camp, Mosiah told the diggers who had flocked around him to get back to work. They were hesitant to go. In Arabic, Grantham assured them that they would not be forced to enter the tomb when they found it. This placated the workers, and they dispersed to their respective duties.

"Mosiah, let me know how they do today. We may have to find some replacements."

"Yes, effendi."

"Let's hope we find the tomb sooner rather than later. I don't want to create any more opportunities for tension."

Thorne, who'd stepped out of the tent to observe Grantham from afar, motioned for his personal guard to stand beside him. He was a hulking, British man who spoke little but followed orders.

"How would you like to make an extra hundred dollars, Cain?"

"What would you like me to do, sir?"

Thorne watched Andoheb getting on a camel. "Follow that man," he said, motioning with his chin. "See where he goes. See if he meets with Spade."

"And if he does, sir?"

"Make sure no one ever sees him again at this expedition site."

"Understood, sir. And if he is not working for Mr. Spade?"

"Same instructions."

"I usually get paid more for these types of tasks, sir."

"But this is just an Egyptian rat."

"Understood, sir."

CHAPTER FOUR

April 9, 1923
Outside of Ancient Memphis,
Egypt

Over the last three days, tensions calmed down. The commotion over Lord Carnarvon's passing had ebbed, and Andoheb had not shown his face since his last visit. The only person who seemed to be upset was Thorne, and he was taking out his frustrations on his long-time butler, Colin, a slightly heavily-built man with a receding hairline. He had recently joined the expedition and had apparently been charged with keeping an eye on Thorne's son, Thomas.

"Damn it, man," Thorne yelled, pacing around the tent. "I gave you simple instructions: stop Thomas from associating with that *girl*. You were supposed to send her away!"

"I'm sorry, Master Thorne," Colin said, biting back a smile. "I tried to send her to Europe, but Master Thomas is very resourceful, and they are a *very* determined couple."

"Nonsense! You just don't have the stomach to deal with this."

He wiped his face with a handkerchief. "Just one more thing I have to take care of when we get home."

"Forgive me, sir."

"That socialist, equality-for-everyone boy of mine has to get it through his thick skull that marriage isn't for *love*—it's a method of advancement! A little *commoner* won't advance his station in society!"

"I understand, sir."

Thorne scowled. "You understand but don't do anything to help me. Go see to my laundry. Even *you* can do that."

"Yes, sir," Colin replied, using his training as a servant to keep from smirking at Thorne. "Thank you, sir."

As Colin walked away, Grantham entered the tent, smiling. "Great news, Mr. Thorne. We found something."

"Is it the tomb?"

"Well, it's not as grandiose as we hoped... it's more like a grave, but at least it conforms to the historical account."

"Take me to it," Thorne demanded.

Grantham led Thorne to the burial site. In the ten-foot hole at the center of the site, Mosiah and another digger stood beside a large, wooden box.

"Not *quite* like what they're finding at the Valley of the Kings," Grantham quipped.

"Let's get it out," Thorne said, impatient. "We have to see what's inside."

Just then, a tremor hit the area, shifting the sands. In the hole, Mosiah and the other digger tried to climb up the ladder, but the rush of the sand quickly overpowered then buried them. When the tremor subsided, Grantham rushed to the hole.

"Oh my God!" he yelled, clawing at the sand with his bare hands.

In Arabic, he ordered the diggers to help him, but they didn't move, worried that the ancient gods were punishing Mosiah and the other digger for uncovering the burial site.

Grantham heard one of them say that this was like what happened at the Tomb of Tutankhamun. He stopped digging and tried to reason with them, but no one would budge. He ran back to the hole, picked up a shovel, and started furiously digging, but he would never be able to save them on his own.

Desperate, he turned to Thorne. "Mr. Thorne! Get your guards and help me dig them out."

"No use. They're already dead."

"You're wrong," he snapped, furious at Thorne's cavalier and bigoted attitude toward Mosiah and the other digger. "There's still a chance."

"By the time I bring the guards back, they will have suffocated."

Grantham gave Thorne a cold stare, wishing it was his patron in that hole. *That would be poetic justice,* he thought.

"Now," Thorne said, clearing his throat. "Let's get rid of these superstitious fools and find some diggers that can bring up that box."

"You can do it without me," Grantham spat.

"I see," Thorne said. "It's up to you, but if you leave this site, I will inform other patrons funding these worldwide expeditions that you are unreliable and lack the commitment necessary to finished the assigned tasks."

Grantham thought for a moment, shooting daggers at Thorne. It wouldn't take much to convince the diggers that Thorne was the one who brought the curse on everyone and let them have fun with him. But that wouldn't bring back Mosiah. He'd been a great assistant and reliable guide all these years.

Grantham gave Thorne a resigned look, realizing he was about to sell his soul.

"I'll get some new diggers."

"Splendid," Thorne said, turning to walk back to the tent. "We'll give your friends a proper Christian burial when we turn them up."

"They're Muslim."

"Christian is what they're going to get."

CHAPTER FIVE

October 15, 1928
Professor Abraham Mueller's House
Just outside Los Angeles, California

In the year since Lilith turned Tori into a vampire at the Universal Studio Opera House, Mueller felt like he'd aged a hundred years. He sighed and sat down to a breakfast cooked by his other project, Frank the Golem.

The process of training them both had been going on for a year. When Mueller built his three-bedroom house outside LA, he'd included a basement expansion with a sturdy, locked cell for the odd days when he couldn't control his lycanthropic transformation into a werewolf.

In the beginning, Tori stayed in there full time, so she could adjust to her powerful, new vampiric urges without harming the innocent people and animals in their local area. In her first days with him, she craved anything that had mammal blood. When Mueller first took her on a tour of the house, she snatched a bird out of the air and sucked it dry. Horrified, but also somewhat impressed, Mueller realized he needed to not only contain her hunger, but also diminish it.

Through his contacts at the hospital, he was able to procure a steady supply of blood for his friend. That continual supply was helpful, but there were still times when she, released from the cell, felt the urge to scour the area for living sources of food. Most times, Mueller and Frank were there to stop her, escort her back to the safe room, and quarantine her until they felt she could safely go out again.

The strategy was working with increasing effectiveness, and the frequency of… *incidents* was going down. However, there were still the odd occasions when Mueller and Frank frantically searched the surrounding city and found Tori hunched over a stray animal, trying to satiate her thirst. It was horrible, even for the two supernatural creatures, to see this young woman, through no fault of her own, being driven to drink the life force of small animals, blood staining her face, hands, and clothes. Mueller was always taken aback by the ferocity of her gaze; in those moments, she was a predator.

Fortunately, her tastes did not extend to humans. Still, Mueller worried that one day, she wouldn't be able to control her urges, and the blood of lower animals would no longer slake her thirst. He'd grown accustomed to carrying a hammer and stake at all times.

Surely enough, Mueller's worries came to fruition. Over the summer, Tori had managed to control her urges for a whole month. She, Mueller, and Frank were having a day out in the city when they picked up on a police chase with their sensitive hearing. The police had uncovered the identity of a serial rapist and were rushing to catch him.

"Let's help them out," Tori said, flying off before Mueller could object.

She followed her senses and saw the suspect running into an

alley. He dove behind a large dumpster and tried to catch his breath.

"Why do they always try to hide in alleys?" she muttered to herself, then swooped into the alley, knocking down the suspect.

"My God, don't hurt me," the man said, scrambling away from Tori. "I'm innocent! They're coming after the wrong man."

Tori thought for a moment, wondering if he was telling the truth. However, an unknown ability started to kick in. "Oh my," she said, sensing his heart rate and other bodily functions. "I can tell you're lying to me. Your body is screaming that out to me. You did everything they accused you of, didn't you?"

"Please show mercy. I don't want to get hanged or castrated."

"Castration," Tori repeated. "Great idea."

Tori transformed fully into a vampire and opened her mouth, revealing her sharp canines. "Your plea has been heard. You won't be hanged."

"Jesus, no," the criminal yelled as Tori lunged for his private area.

Mueller and Frank followed Tori into the alley but stopped short when they saw what she had done. The rapist, in shock and losing a lot of blood, was dead.

"What have you done, Mistress Tori?" Frank asked.

"Dispensed justice," Tori said, wiping her mouth. "He did what he was accused of."

"The police are a block away," Mueller said. "We've got to get out of here."

"See you at the house," Tori said, starting to fly off.

Mueller and Frank darted away, struggling to keep up with the whims of the young vampire. "You know, Frank, training you was so much more fun."

"Thank you."

Tori also had difficulties, despite once being a Temporal Guardian, adjusting to life in the 1920's. There would be times when she would mumble within the hearing range of an annoyed Mueller about how she missed conveniences like a microwave or the internet. When Mueller took her to the Los Angeles Public Library, she was aghast at having to use a card catalog. "God, this takes too long," she said. While concerts were wonderful, she did not care much for the movies of the period, calling many of the silent films, "corny, unsophisticated, and predictable." Permanently wearing the clothing of the period also did not appeal to her more modern fashion sensibilities. Finally, even though she had no craving for human food, she had the occasional memory of how good McDonald's french fries were or the taste of chicken wings from the Native Grill and Wings restaurant in Tempe.

Training the Golem proved to be easier, especially since he did not have the same… *cravings* as Tori. Mueller and Tori, when she was able, raised Frank like a small child. They taught him to speak, read, and perform tasks around the house. He was no longer just a big, reanimated bodyguard made of clay. On a good day, Tori went on a shopping trip and procured a medium tan, Mediterranean foundation for Frank's skin. She considered going the full nine yards and buying him a full face of makeup but wound up sticking to just the foundation and an eyebrow pencil. She also got him a new wig. The original one, in her mind, made him look like Uncle Fester from *Addams Family Values*. In essence, he was like a butler who looked like, to Tori, a cross of Boris Karloff's Frankenstein's Monster and Arnold Schwarzenegger's The Terminator.

The educational experience of teaching the Golem also helped Tori take her mind off adjusting to her new condition. Every day, she would have Frank sit in a mock class setting in the basement to learn the alphabet, basic words, and addition and subtraction. Tori would remember her own kindergarten and first grade experiences when Frank would forget carrying over numbers when adding or subtracting multi-number problems. *Jeez*, she thought one time.

The blind man in the Bride of Frankenstein had it easier than me.

They even had to go through a discussion when giving him a name. Remembering the creature from Mary Shelley's *Frankenstein*, one of the many books they'd read aloud to him, Muller asked the Golem if he would like the name "Frank."

"But that was not the name of the creature," the Golem said. "In the Frankenstein book you read, he suggested being called Adam."

"That's true," Tori said. "Would you like to be called Adam instead?"

The Golem considered for a moment. He thought back to the passages of Genesis Tori had read to him and managed a small smile. "There is only one Adam. I'll be Frank."

On the morning of October 15, 1928, Frank unlocked Tori's cell. She had gone another full week without Abraham or Frank having to go out and look for her.

"Good morning, Mistress," Frank said. "You look good."

"Thank you, Frank," Tori, wearing a Victorian Nightgown, replied. "I think I've made another turn for the better. Hopefully, this will last longer."

"Each time, it has, Mistress."

"Let's see what he's up today."

Mueller, dressed in a brown, tweed suit to go to the university, was sitting at the breakfast table, reading the morning edition of the Los Angeles Times. He had some toast with jelly and butter for breakfast. Across from him, there was a bowl set out for Tori.

"Good morning," Tori, still in her nightgown, said, coming into the dining room.

"Good morning. How are you feeling?"

"I was telling Frank I think I've made a turn."

"That's good."

Tori sat by her bowl and looked at the mixture of blood and oatmeal. "This is different."

"Frank and I thought we could try to train you into eating some normal food alongside your daily supply."

"Is that even possible?"

"I don't know," Mueller replied. "We'll see."

She took a spoon and scooped up some oatmeal tinged with blood. She put it in her mouth and immediately spit it out across the table. Her face turned red, and she looked away.

Mueller wiped a speck of oatmeal off his suit jacket and gave Tori a gentle smile. "It's okay," he said, holding her arm. "This may take time. Frank, please get the Mistress a bottle of what I brought home last night."

"Yes, Master Abraham."

"It'll be alright, Tori. It's still better than going out and eating a dozen rats."

Tori sighed. "True. I guess this is all still one day at a time."

"Precisely. You know, this is going a lot better than I thought it would."

"Thank you." Tori eyed the slight bulge in Mueller's jacket. "But you still carry a hammer and stake when you and Frank go on your search and rescue missions."

"Only as a last resort."

Frank brought a bottle of blood for Tori, who drank it.

"That hit the spot. Thank you, Frank." She looked at Mueller and giggled.

"What are you laughing at?"

"Just the daily reminder that you need to brush the toast crumbs out of your beard before you go to the university."

"Thank you."

"What are you doing today?" Tori asked.

"Well, I'm lecturing at the university during the day, as you know. Afterward, I'm going to the Natural History Museum of Los Angeles County."

"That's great. Can you take me?"

"I don't know if that's a great idea," Mueller replied. "You haven't been around that many people at once since you came here. The urge may be too great."

"I promise I'll be good, and if I can't control myself, I'll tell you and we can leave."

Mueller thought for a moment. "Alright. We'll try it." He gave Tori a reassuring smile. "Go out with Frank later and get a dress for the event. The invitation says it's black tie."

Tori rose from her chair and rushed to hug Mueller. "Thank you so much. I won't let you down."

"I know you believe that," Mueller said, embracing Tori. "You'll understand that, as a precaution, I still have to bring the equipment."

"I understand. What time is the event?"

"Eight o'clock. I'll pick you up after my lecture. I should be home by five."

"Great. What are we seeing today?"

"An ancient Egyptian exhibit, including the mummy of the Aten Priest, Sennefer."

"A mummy," Tori said. "I used to love those movies when I was a kid. I used to go with my friends from school and The Foundation, though that last one with Tom Cruise and Russell Crowe really sucked."

Mueller gave Tori a bewildered expression—he had no idea what she was talking about. He looked at Frank, who could not offer any help.

Tori smiled at both of them. "Very sorry. Too much information from my past life in the future. Maybe you guys are familiar with the ones with Boris Karloff and Lon Chaney?"

Again, Mueller gave Tori a non-plussed look.

"That's right," Tori said, frowning. "Those haven't happened yet either."

"Oh," Mueller said. "I understand now. Try not to talk about the future again. Don't want to accidentally disrupt the timeline."

"It's hard. I miss my friends from my time and the work at The Foundation. I also…"

"Oh, don't go talking again about how much you miss the fried potatoes at McDougal's."

"You mean french fries at McDonald's?" Tori asked Mueller. "I'm sorry. How long did it take you to stop making references to all the people you've known through the millennia? Or get used to a world you did not grow up in?"

Mueller smiled. "It took a while, but I had the advantage of actually living through history."

"Anyway," Tori said, brushing the topic aside, "you said a priest of Aten. That means he worked for the Pharoah Akhenaten when Egypt experimented with monotheism."

"That's right," Mueller said. "That Foundation of yours gave you an excellent education."

"There were scholars from my time who speculated Moses was associated with that group. Care to confirm?"

"What did I just say about polluting the timeline?"

"*Fine*," Tori said. "This priest of Aten. Was he a friend?"

"Not exactly," Mueller replied. "I'm the one who sort of mummified then buried him."

CHAPTER SIX

October 15, 1928
Natural History Museum of Los Angeles County
8:30 p.m.

The black-tie evening event showcasing the mummy of the Aten Priest, Sennefer, at the Natural History Museum of Los Angeles County was attended by many archeology academics from the local universities. There was also a sizable press contingent to cover the event. The museum director, John Sommers, made sure that everyone was comfortable in the reception area, their thirst for alcohol quenched and their hunger satisfied with hors d'oeuvres.

If those were the only people at the event, Thorne would have been totally pleased. Unfortunately, Grantham was there to share the limelight because he had led the expedition. Since the day when the two diggers perished, the men had hardly spoken to one another, with Grantham preferring to exchange communications with Thorne through either Colin, Thorne's butler, Thomas, his son, or Agatha, his daughter.

To make matters worse, Director Sommers told him that

his archeological rival, Spade, would be in attendance to give his perspective as a guest Egyptologist.

There were also those anonymous letters that said Thorne would pay for desecrating Egypt's ancient dead and mistreating its people. Out of caution, Thorne hired an extra bodyguard to work alongside Cain and trail him throughout the evening.

His stress didn't end there. Agatha, who was at the event for appearance's sake, was hardly speaking to him. She was angry that he didn't bail her out for two days when she was arrested during a women's equal rights and worker safety protest. Worse than that, Thomas showed up drunk, after having been on a drinking binge the whole day. He was consumed with mourning the death of the girl he loved. He blamed Thorne for her suicide, claiming that the forced separation broke her heart and drove her to it.

Thorne brushed the whole incident aside; it just proved how weak and lowly the girl really was. Thorne ordered Colin to keep an eye on the children, so they would not embarrass the family name at this important event.

Tori and Abraham walked into the event together. He was dressed in a classic, black-tie tuxedo. She wore a dark red, sleeveless, drop-waist gown with a deep V down the back and a large bow cinching the waist at her lower back. She'd paired it with matching shoes and had neatly styled her hair with curls and finger waves to match the fashion sensibilities of the time.

Tori looked around in awe. "This kind of looks like an event from Downton Abbey."

"Downton Abbey," Mueller repeated. "What's that?"

"Sorry, did it again," Tori said, looking back at Mueller, noticing for the first time how handsome he looked in the well-tailored tuxedo. "You look good in that tux, Abraham."

"Thank you," Abraham responded, taking in Tori's appearance. "You look very elegant. You and Frank did a great job picking out that dress."

"Thank you," Tori said, adjusting her hair. "That might be the nicest thing you've said to me since we met."

"Really?" Abraham said, a little taken aback. "I'll learn to be better at sharing my positive thoughts with you."

Tori smiled. "So, where is the mummy?"

"First, they're going to try and get us in the mood by giving us lots of liquor and food. Then we'll have to suffer," Abraham cleared his throat, "I mean, go through what will hopefully be an entertaining presentation. I suspect we won't see Sennefer for about an hour or so." He looked at Tori intently. "How are you feeling?"

"Fine."

"Remember, let me know if things get too much for you."

"Not a problem," she said, holding up her purse. "I brought a little flask of what you brought over from the coroner's office last night."

"Good. I see him," Abraham said.

"Who?"

"Malcom Thorne, the industrialist who funded the expedition. He's talking to Trevor Grantham, the leader of the dig." Abraham frowned. "He's flanked by two bodyguards. He must be getting twice the threats he's used to getting."

"Not a very popular fellow," Tori said.

"Total ass," Mueller said. "Around the time of the war, I had dealings with people who had less than satisfactory experiences with him, to put it mildly."

Tori looked over at Thorne and Grantham. She could see from their body language that the two were not on the best of terms. "You don't need enhanced senses to know those two hate each other."

After Grantham left Thorne, a slender, dark-haired man wearing a white tuxedo and holding a note pad approached him.

"Can I help you?" Thorne asked.

"Good evening, Mr. Thorne. I'm William Richardson with the Los Angeles Herald."

"This isn't the time for reporter questions, young man."

"But sir, I'll be brief. Can you just comment on the fear that the mummy of Sennefer and the Eye of Aten carry a dangerous curse?"

"Nonsense! I'm still here. My expedition leader is still alive and well. My daughter and son are still here. There's nothing to that curse poppycock," Thorne said, shaking his head.

"But your daughter was just arrested and spent a night in jail, sir, and there are reports that your son's former girlfriend took her own life. That seems like a family that may be plagued by a curse."

"Nonsense," Thorne said, dismissing the claim with a hand gesture. "Just unfortunate coincidences. No curse working its way there."

"I see," Richardson said writing down what Thorne said and thinking that the millionaire's dismissive comments about the misfortune of his family would make good print. "And what about the diggers who died when the burial site was found?"

"An unfortunate accident," Thorne said. "There isn't a day that goes by that I don't think about those unfortunate souls, but it was simply an accident."

"You didn't have that attitude when the Egyptian government made you pay a settlement to those diggers' families for unsafe working conditions."

"Enough!" Thorne said, shooting Richardson a nasty look. "I have guests to meet. I'll have one of the attendants see you out."

"Hold on a minute," Richardson said, reaching into his jacket. "I have an invite from the museum curator for my paper."

"It's just been withdrawn," Thorne said, yanking the notepad out of Richardson's hand.

"Hey!" Richardson protested. "That's my property."

Thorne and his bodyguards pushed Richardson aside

and walked away. When they were, gone, Richardson took out another notepad.

Thorne noticed that Reverend John Sullivan, the face of Savior Front Radio, reputed anti-Communist and anti-Semite, and his good friend, had arrived at the event.

He approached the radio personality and clasped his hand. "Good to see you, Reverend. I'm looking forward to being on your show tomorrow and attending the rally afterwards."

"Likewise, Mr. Thorne," Sullivan said. "We need to keep that liberal Hoover in line."

Thorne laughed and patted the reverend on the shoulder. "You have a great time this evening, and come see me before you go."

Thorne's mood shifted back toward the negative when he saw his son at the bar. *Where's that worthless Colin when I need him?* Thorne approached the bar but was intercepted by his daughter and one of her friends from the Women's Rights Movement. They were both dressed well for the party, but Thorne was distressed by the very visible Women's Rights Movement pins they were wearing.

"Well, father, is this the event you hoped it would be?" Agatha said, taking a sip of champagne.

"Not now, Agatha," Thorne said, trying to get past her. "Thomas is getting drunk again."

"Who can blame him after what you did?" Agatha said, not moving out of the way.

"Oh, go and be with Grantham. I understand that is one of your favorite *pastimes* these days."

Agatha gave Thorne an indignant look. "At least Trevor is a real man with a heart."

"Who still takes my money."

Agatha rolled her eyes. "Before you go, may I introduce Ava Perez, one of my sisters in the local Women's Rights Movement?" She glared at Thorne. "You had her arrested with me and thrown in jail after last week's protest."

"I wish I could say I'm pleased to meet you, Ms. Perez."

"Same here," she responded.

"One word of free advice," Thorne said, leaning in. "Stay away from my daughter at these events. You never know when the police will have to detain her and the people with her again." Thorne smirked. "Also, keep in mind that the officers might be harsher with someone of your race."

"You son of a..." Ava started to say.

Thorne growled and brushed Agatha and her friend aside.

"Your father is a real schmuck," Ava said, watching him approach Thomas.

"Don't feel singled out," Agatha said. "My father is that way with anyone who is not a rich white man."

Thorne put his hand on Thomas's shoulder. He was 22 and seemed to grow taller and broader every day, even despite his recent tendencies.

"You really need to stop the drinking. You'll kill yourself."

"Maybe that's what I want," Thomas said, finishing his drink. "Then I'll be with her. But you wouldn't understand that, *Dad*, seeing as you were the one who drove her to her death." He swiveled to look at Thorne, shrugging his hand away.

"Control yourself," Thorne said, stepping closer to Thomas. "You'll make a spectacle of yourself."

"Oh, now we know what you *really* care about," Thomas replied. "You don't want the heir-apparent to embarrass his father on his big day. Well, don't worry about that. I'll slink off to a quiet corner with this nice bottle of scotch I have inside my jacket."

"When will you realize that I did you a *favor* by getting rid of that girl?"

"You're scum, Dad. You always have been."

Thomas walked away, and Thorne looked around for his

lawyer. His eyes finally landed on Cartwright, whose tail coat accentuated his tall, slender, elderly frame. They made eye contact, and Cartwright, who had been discreetly watching the exchange, approached Throne.

"I see that didn't go well, Malcom."

"But not unexpected, Blake. Are the new will and Grantham's dismissal papers prepared?"

"Yes."

"Good, I'll sign those first thing tomorrow morning. I'm going to teach those idiot kids and ungrateful archeologist lessons they won't forget. By the way, do you know that reporter that's here, Richardson at the Herald?"

"I've read some of his work," Cartwright replied. "Very good writer."

"Too bad," Thorne said. "Call the Herald tomorrow and have him fired. He's too rude to be a newspaperman."

"I'll see to it." Cartwright cleared his throat. "I saw you talking to Reverend Sullivan. Are you sure about going on his radio show? He's a bit... *raw.*"

"He's a means to an end—if Hoover doesn't completely destroy the country, working with Sullivan will help me get the base audience I need for the 1932 election. Our future president is almost like a socialist. He'll give *everything* away to the people."

"Still, I think there's some risk going on that radio show. You don't want our financial backers like Schwartz and Epstein to call in our loans."

"Screw those kike bastards. We'll get Ford, Rockefeller, or Carnegie-Mellon to come in as backers. They're tied in with us now on The Utopia Program, so they'll join up."

"Understood," Cartwright said, sensing it would be unwise to keep pushing the issue. "I'm just trying to look out for you."

Thorne sighed. "What would I do without you, Blake?"

Tori and Abraham overheard Thorne's conversation.

Tori shook her head. "He sure knows how to win friends and influence people."

"Unfortunately, he can afford to be a bastard."

"And associate with vermin like that anti-Semitic apostate Reverend Sullivan," Tori said.

A waiter approached with a tray. Tori and Abraham paused their conversation, smiled, and each took a flute of champagne.

"Force of habit," Tori said, looking at the glass. "I'll go for my private stock in a little bit."

Mueller chuckled. "It's okay. It's good to mask your appetites."

They turned their attention to Richardson and watched him make the rounds with the guests. "He's a persistent one," Tori admiringly said. "He's going to get as much as he can before they throw him out."

"I've dealt with him on some of the cases I've consulted on."

"Even the one with us and Lilith last year?"

"Yes. He gives new meaning to persistence."

"Before I forget," Tori said. "This morning you said you 'sort of' mummified Sennefer. What does that mean?"

"There wasn't time to do the full mummification process, so I went to a known contact while General Nakhtmin and his men were ransacking Memphis and had the body bandaged before we buried him in a wooden box in the desert."

"No sarcophagus either?"

"Nope."

Richardson looked around the room for someone who could provide an enticing interview for his article before he was ejected. He watched a tall man with a dark complexion enter the room. The museum director addressed him as Mr. Spade, and, hearing that name, Richardson rushed to meet the new guest.

Abraham followed Richardson's trail and was shocked to

recognize the tall man.

"Speak of the devil."

Tori saw the concerned look on his face. "What is it? What's wrong?" She followed his gaze. "Do you know that man?"

"Come with me," Abraham replied.

Richardson was pestering Spade with the same questions he had posed to Thorne. At least the new guest was giving juicy answers, suggesting he was open to the possibility of curses bestowed by the ancient Egyptians.

"So, you believe in the mummy's curse or vengeance, Mr. Spade?" Richardson asked while taking notes.

"I believe we shouldn't…" Spade trailed off when Abraham joined the conversation.

"You were saying?" Abraham said, smiling at Spade.

The Egyptologist, quickly trying to recompose his thoughts, smiled back at Abraham. "I was saying, Mr. Richardson, that we shouldn't discount the possibility of curses just because science has yet to acknowledge their existence and power."

"Thank you, Mr. Spade," Richardson said. "Is there anything else you would—"

"Not right now," Spade said, stepping closer to Mueller and whispering in his ear, "It's been a long time, Abram."

"And you too, General Nakhtmin."

Tori, with her enhanced hearing, dropped her jaw. *The murderer and the grave digger here to pay their respects after over 3,000 years,* she thought to herself. *This is going to be a fun evening.*

Chapter Seven

"You've actually got some grey hairs, General," Abraham said. "And you've grown a beard," Spade said. "So, what do you call yourself these days?"

"Abraham Mueller… and you're now Julian Spade."

Tori made a small grunting sound in a move to get attention. "Sorry, I just had to clear my throat."

Spade smiled. "And who is your young friend?"

"Victoria Jacobsen."

"Is she one of us?" Spade asked.

"Not exactly," Abraham replied. "She is one of Lilith's."

"Really? Sounds like an interesting story."

As the trio started to converse further, Thorne, trailed by his two bodyguards, came upon them. He was not happy to see Spade. "I think you showing up here on my big day is bad form, Spade."

"Sommers invited me as an expert on the period," Spade replied in an even tone. "I'm not here to take away from your glory, if that's what you're worried about."

"Liar," Thorne retorted. "You're here to upstage me. Well, you won't get the chance. I'll find Sommers and have him throw you out."

"You're being rude in front of my friends, Malcom. I think you should go."

Thorne looked at Tori and Mueller like he was seeing them for the first time. Realizing this was not the best time to confront his rival, he snarled at Spade then walked away.

"Not a nice fellow," Spade said.

"So, I've discovered," Tori said.

"He works hard at being an ass," Spade quipped.

Tori and Abraham laughed.

"Ms. Jacobsen, would you mind excusing Abraham and me for a few minutes? We have a lot to catch up on."

Tori looked at Abraham for approval.

"Go ahead and mingle," he said, smiling. "Come find me if you need anything."

Tori nodded and went off into the crowd. She tried to sip her champagne, but when she brought it up to her mouth, she wrinkled her nose. "Nah," she said to herself. "I'll just have to settle for the iron supplement in the flask."

Richardson saw Tori talking to Spade and Mueller and thought she might be a good person to interview. Her being attractive was also a point in her favor. He came up to her and smiled. "Can I get you an hors d'oeuvre, Miss...?"

"Jacobsen," Tori replied. "And no, I'm not hungry for those."

"A drink then?"

Tori held up her still-full glass of champagne. "You're not a very observant man."

Richardson laughed. "I'm sorry. I'm always awkward when I meet attractive women."

"What a line," Tori replied a little sarcastically. "What can I do for you, Mr. Richardson?"

"You know who I am?" Richardson tried not to let his excitement show through.

"My friend Abraham mentioned you had interviewed him before for your newspaper."

"Professor Mueller, yes. On some of the more bizarre cases to hit the county the last couple of years."

"That's what he told me."

"Right," Richardson replied. "I saw you speaking with Mueller, Spade, and Thorne. May I ask what you were all talking about?"

"I'm afraid not," Tori said, smiling. "That's private between the three of us."

"Okay," Richardson said. "May I ask what you think of coming to see the exhibit this evening?"

"I think it's interesting," Tori said. Her face lit up. "I'm a big fan of history."

"Do you think there's anything to the idea that a mummy's curse could take vengeance on the people who found and dug up the burial site of Sennefer and the Eye of Aten?"

"Maybe. I have the same mindset as Spade. Quoting Shakespeare, 'there's more things on heaven and Earth than are dreamt in your philosophy.'"

"Exactly," Richardson replied, thinking he had made a connection with a kindred spirit.

"Or this could be more sensationalism for young reporters like you to get more people to buy your paper and increase your notoriety."

"No, I am all about uncovering hidden truths," Richardson honestly replied. "Like Mueller told you, there has been some weird stuff happening here in the last year. We had that cult pretending they were vampires."

"I heard," Tori responded, thinking about how those same

events indirectly caused her... condition.

"Yes. The police covered up that one. Now we have a mummy exhibit with a supposed curse on it. Scary, isn't it?"

"Maybe if it were true," Tori said. "The key word being *if*."

Before Richardson could ask another question, Tori gave him her glass of champagne. "I'm not thirsty for this. Can you put it away for me? I have to go to the powder room and take a drink of my private stock."

"Of course. May I call on you later?"

Tori smiled at Richardson. "I'm not a source for one of your articles."

"I didn't mean for that," Richardson said, looking a little flushed.

"Oh," Tori said. "You can if you want to. It might be fun if you're not just trying to dig up your next scoop."

"Excellent, and I won't be. I'll call tomorrow. What's your number?"

"Mueller's in the book. I'm staying with him for now."

"Oh," Richardson, said, a little disappointed. "Are you and he together?"

"Not that way."

"Great," he replied, smiling. "I mean, understood. Talk to you later."

"Most likely," Tori responded, walking away. She smiled to herself, but only when she was sure Richardson wasn't looking.

Overjoyed, Richardson drank Tori's glass, put it back at the bar, and went back to hunting for more potential interview candidates.

Spade and Mueller moved to the terrace, so they could have a more private conversation.

"How long has it been?" Spade asked.

"I don't know. American Civil War?"

"That's right. Gettysburg. We were working for Union Intelligence." Spade shook his head. "Those were dangerous times for this country."

"We pulled through. Now tell me what you're *really* doing here."

"The Eye. I need it to rid me of this curse."

Abraham raised his eyebrows. "You've had enough of immortality?"

"I'm very tired. I've had enough of being a part of the human condition. All we do is advance technologically to become better killers and inflict suffering on others."

"I don't know," Abraham said. "I think there's been social growth over the last few centuries. The Renaissance. The Enlightenment. Democracy and Republics."

"Imperialism," Spade replied. "Extreme Nationalism, Social Darwinism, a World War, and this latest trend Mussolini is leading. I've had it, Abraham."

"So, you've come to the end of the road. Why didn't you dig up the Eye for yourself?" Abraham glanced at Spade. "I would have told you where we buried Sennefer."

"I tried finding you, but I had no luck. I love the irony that you're here tonight. Help me get the Eye."

"Hold on," Mueller said. "I'm not becoming an art thief. Besides, you need more than just the Eye to remove the curse. You need the words to go with it."

Spade flashed Mueller a grin. "Already obtained. When Horemheb's tomb was discovered, we were able to get the hieroglyph tablets with the prayer to remove the curse. The tomb looked like it had been ransacked by robbers through the centuries, so it was easy for my people to fleece the tablet before any serious cataloguing was done."

"And now you need Thorne to let you borrow the Eye to complete the ritual?" Abraham sighed. "Like *that's* ever going to happen."

"Exactly. Think, Abraham. This might also help you. The Eye

can do more than just inflict and remove curses. Back then, the Atenists said that the Eye had tremendous wish-granting powers. Those prayers might be able to remove the curse Elohim placed on you. You've suffered far longer than I have."

Abraham thought for a moment. He hadn't considered this possibility. Could the Eye really help Tori escape the vampiric existence Lilith inflicted on her? He looked at Spade. "Let me think for a little while, General."

"Very well," he said, patting Mueller on the shoulder. "But don't take too long. We don't have much time to take advantage of this opportunity."

Spade left the terrace, leaving Abraham to think about the General's proposal. *Could this be the key to releasing me and Tori from the torturous existences we've had to endure?*

A few moments later, Mueller heard screams in the reception room. He whirled around and plunged into darkness. All the lights had gone out. People were frantic and bumping into each other. With his sensitive canine hearing, Mueller heard a man scream from a room on the other side of the reception area. He transformed his eyes to canine form and weaved across the room to investigate. His journey was complicated by the many confused people getting in his way, but he eventually made it across the room. He opened the door to a small office. It was still dark, but he could still see Thorne's body lying on the white, tile floor. He could also see the person standing over his body. It was Tori.

CHAPTER EIGHT

October 15, 1928
Natural History Museum of Los Angeles County
A little after 9:00 p.m.

Abraham looked at Tori and reached for the hammer and stake in his breast pocket. He never really thought she would succumb to her vampiric urges.

"Tori, what have you done?"

"ME?" Tori shot back, indignant. "I heard a scream from the reception area and got here seconds before you did. It's Thorne and one of his bodyguards."

Abraham let go of the hammer and stake in his breast pocket and went to look at the bodies. He knelt beside Thorne's first and examined his neck. There was no blood and no bite marks, but his neck was broken, and there was a piece of cloth next to it. He stood up and went to examine the bodyguard. His body was lying on the other side of a coffee table and was in the same state as Thorne's. No bite marks, no blood, a broken neck, and another piece of cloth. He smiled and looked at his friend.

"Thank goodness," Abraham said, breathing a sigh of relief. "I'm sorry I jumped to conclusions."

"I forgive you," Tori said. "What do you think of the strips of cloth?"

Abraham was careful not to touch anything to avoid contaminating the crime scene. "It looks like linen."

"The type used in mummification?" Tori asked.

Abraham considered Tori's question. "What you're suggesting is something I haven't seen in my approximately seven millennia of existence."

"But not impossible like werewolves, vampires, and golems aren't impossible."

Abraham smiled at her. "Point taken. We need to call Carl at the police department."

The lights came back on. A minute later, Agatha and Grantham, trying to slip away from the party, burst into the room.

Agatha gasped. "My God!" She turned away and hugged Grantham.

"Where the hell are the bodyguards?" Grantham asked.

"One of them is over here," Tori replied, pointing at the bodyguard Thorne had just hired.

"I'll get the others," Agatha said. "Stay with them, my darling."

Grantham stared at Tori and Abraham, who returned the gesture. Tori, looking to break the tension, asked, "What do you think of the party?"

"I think it just got better," Grantham said.

Agatha led Ava, Thomas, Colin, Cartwright, Richardson, and Sommers into the room.

"My God. What did you two do to them?" Thomas asked. He started to rush Tori and Abraham but was pulled back by Colin and Cartwright.

"Control yourself, Thomas," Cartwright said, struggling. "You're the head of the family now. Show some restraint and maturity."

"They didn't do it," Sommers said. "This is Professor Mueller from the University of California. He's a criminologist. They must have found the bodies first."

Richardson glanced at the linen on the floor by Thorne's neck. "My God, it's true. The mummy has risen and killed Thorne." He couldn't contain himself. "Just think of the headline. The Mummy's Vengeance Strikes Again," he said, gesturing along with his fantasy.

Abraham walked up to Richardson and grabbed him by his collar. "Shut up," he said. "I don't want to stir up any panic or hysteria." He let go of Richardson and faced the group. "This is an active crime scene, and I don't want to see any foolish behavior. Now, where is the other bodyguard?"

No one had an answer.

Grantham had a revelation. "The exhibits! Did they steal the exhibits?"

"How can you think about that right now?" Thomas asked.

"Sommers and Grantham," Abraham said. "Take me to the exhibit. Tori, use the phone in here to call Detective Bell at the police station, and tell him what's happened. Don't touch the body or disturb the crime scene. Everyone else, get out of here until the police come and ask for you. Tori, stay here and watch over the crime scene."

"You got it" Tori replied, thinking to herself this was like being in an episode of *The X Files*.

Sommers led Grantham and Abraham to the exhibit, but the mummy of Sennefer and the Eye of Aten were gone.

"The plot thickens," Abraham said. "It looks like the blackout served two purposes. Joseph, make sure no one leaves the museum."

Abraham noticed two more pieces of linen at the base of Sennefer's display.

"You don't suppose," Sommers said, eyeing the linen,

"Richardson's right with his idea about the mummy's vengeance?"

"They have the Eye of Aten now," Grantham said. "If they somehow have the prayers of the Aten Priests and know what to do with them, they could control immense power."

"In the end," Abraham said, "while we shouldn't discount anything, I think we'll find that the culprit—or culprits—are very human. The criminal is likely someone who was in the reception room and whose accomplice did the dirty work. The pieces of linen are likely an attempt at misdirection. That aside, I need to find the other bodyguard. Also, where's Spade?"

"He was in the reception room when the lights came on."

"Glad to hear it," Abraham said, surprised that the number one suspect in his mind was still here. *He could have had an accomplice though. He's powerful and resourceful enough. Then again, it could be anyone in that reception room. They all had the means, and Thorne was not liked at all.*

CHAPTER NINE

Detective Carl Bell and the coroner, Dr. Scott Morris, arrived with half a dozen police officers thirty minutes after Tori called. Abraham went over what happened and what they did to secure the crime scene and the two bodies.

"It's never a dull moment with you, Bram," Bell said, exhausted from a long day at work. "Last year, vampires, and now, a mummy's curse."

"What can I say? I bring excitement to the job."

Bell laughed and advised his sergeant to secure the reception hall. No one was allowed to leave without giving a statement.

"You," Tori interjected, "should concentrate on his family members, the expedition leader, the butler, and the rival Egyptologist. They all have an axe to grind with Thorne."

"I intend to, Miss Jacobsen," Bell replied, trying to hide his annoyance. "But we shouldn't narrow our possible list of suspects just yet."

"Before I forget," Tori said, "the Thorne lawyer is here."

"Hopefully, he won't be too obstructive," Bell said, thinking back to a few troublesome witnesses.

Abraham joined Morris, as he examined Thorne's body. Two policemen took pictures of the bodies and the crime scene and combed the area for clues. Anyone entering the crime scene was vetted and put on a pair of gloves.

"What's this?" Morris asked. He used a pair of tweezers to hold up the piece of linen.

"Mummy linen," Abraham replied.

Morris frowned. "Oh, come on, Abraham. I can see this is what the killer used to help strangle and break the victim's neck. Nothing supernatural about that."

"Perhaps," Abraham said.

"We found another piece of linen by the bodyguard," Tori said. "Why would a killer bring two pieces of linen?"

"Maybe just to fool people into thinking that a mummy did it," Morris replied, taking off his gloves and adjusting his spectacles. "Well, let's get these two to the morgue. Abraham, you want to join me there and assist?"

"Delighted. I just want to speak with someone before I go. Give me a few minutes, and we can drive together."

Abraham turned to Bell. "Carl, is it okay for Tori to stay with you during the suspect interviews, while I go with Scott to the morgue? She was here tonight and can provide additional, trustworthy perspective."

Bell's face fell. "Oh, come on, Bram," he whispered. "I don't have time for amateur hour, and your friend has a habit of telling me how to do my job. Besides, what if the chief comes in during the interviews? I might catch a bunch of shit."

"Oh, I'll smooth things over with him. Just tell him to call me." Abraham put his hand on Bell's shoulder. "Trust me on this. I think she'll be of great assistance."

Bell sighed. "Okay, but you owe me big time if this blows up in my face."

"Understood. I'll tell her to behave. Is it okay if I chat with Spade, the rival Egyptologist, before I take off? He's an old friend."

"Sure," Bell replied. "But let's compare notes on what he says to both of us."

Abraham pulled Tori aside and briefed her on what was going to happen. "Now, while I'm gone, help Carl out, but *behave*. Remember, he's the lead detective."

"Naturally," Tori said, imitating Rosalind Russel at the end of *Auntie Mame.*

"Good," Abraham said, not sure how Tori and Carl working together would turn out. "How are you doing otherwise?" He gave Tori a meaningful look.

"Oh, I'm fine. I took a drink from the flask before I heard the scream. The excitement of this case is taking up all my attention. It's like I am in middle of an Arthur Conan Doyle or Agatha Christie mystery." She grinned. "Did you know that Doyle wrote a story about a living mummy?"

"I think I've read that one, yes," Abraham said, giving Tori a smile. "I'm going to talk to Spade before I go with Scott. Remember, *behave.*"

"Of course," Tori said, grinning again.

Abraham went to the reception area and found Spade talking to Sommers.

Before he could reach them, Richardson, his pencil and note pad at the ready, sidled up to Abraham. "Professor, can you tell me anything?"

"Not now. Maybe tomorrow."

"Is it true the Eye of Aten and the Mummy have been stolen?"

"Don't stir up any hysteria," Abraham said, giving Richardson a stern look. "We don't need to cause panic in the community."

"You got it," Richardson replied. "No problem there."

Abraham did not believe Richardson, but he realized that aside from killing him, there was little he could do to stop him from writing what he wanted to write. He pulled Spade aside, and Sommers moved away to join Grantham and Agatha.

"Walk with me," Abraham said, leading Spade to a corner of the room. "Tell me this isn't you."

"I swear, Abraham. I did not kill those men or steal anything," Spade said, looking Abraham in the eye.

"Did you hire anyone to do it for you?" Abraham said, meeting Spade's gaze.

"No!"

"I hope you're not lying," Abraham said, finally looking away. "I wouldn't want us on opposite sides. It won't end well."

"You have nothing to worry about," Spade said. "I want to help you find them. Let me know what I can do."

"We'll talk later," Abraham replied, satisfied with Spade's responses for the moment. "The detective and my friend, Miss Jacobsen, will question you later. Don't leave."

"Of course."

After Thorne and the bodyguard's bodies were removed, Bell had two of his men set up an interview station in the same room with three chairs and a table.

"May I suggest we start with the attorney?" Tori said, sitting down next to Bell. "He should have the most background information on everyone that had a strong motive to kill Thorne."

"Good idea," Bell replied. "I was just thinking about that. If something comes to you during the interviews, just whisper it in my ear."

"Very well," Tori replied, thinking, *I hope I can handle*

whispering so close to his jugular.

Bell told one of his men to bring Cartwright in.

"Thank you for speaking with us, Mr. Cartwright," Bell said.

"Absolutely. Anything I can do to help."

"Thank you," Bell said, taking out his pencil and notepad. "The first question I have is where were you when the lights went off just before 9:00 p.m.?"

"I was in the reception room with everyone else. It was very chaotic and confusing."

"Was there anyone you were with specifically?" Tori asked.

Bell stared at her. It was a good enough question, but he was supposed to be leading the investigation.

"I was with Reverend Sullivan."

"When was the last time you saw Mr. Thorne?" Bell asked.

"We were both at the bar. His bodyguard, Cain, came over and whispered something in his ear. He said he had to go, and they both left."

"What time was that?" Bell asked.

"A moment or two before the lights went out."

"Did you see them come in here?"

"No, I wasn't paying attention at that point."

"Did you or the others hear anything before Miss Thorne came to get you?"

"No, it was too noisy in the reception room for me, at least."

"I see," Bell said. "Do you know who might have wanted to kill Mr. Thorne?"

"Do you want the long or short list?" Cartwright said, giving Bell a wry smile. "Malcom Thorne was a very powerful man with interests around the world. You don't get that way without upsetting a few people."

"Including guests at this evening's event?"

"Including them, Detective."

"How about Mr. Grantham, the expedition leader?" Bell asked. "Did he have a reason to kill Mr. Thorne?"

Cartwright nodded. "He was about to be dismissed."

"Why?" Bell asked.

"Mr. Thorne had grown tired of his methods. He wanted someone with less—"

"Attention to safety protocols?" Tori interjected.

Bell gave her a cold stare.

"That could be one interpretation," Cartwright replied.

"How about his children?" Bell asked. "Did they have reason to kill Mr. Thorne?"

"I'm afraid I can't go into that. I am the family lawyer as well as the lead counsel for Thorne Industries. I am constrained by attorney-client privilege."

Tori leaned towards Bell to whisper in his ear. When she got close to his neck, the warmth of his blood seemed to call to her. *Control yourself, Tori.* She whispered, "I'll take that as a yes."

Bell nodded. "With Mr. Thorne deceased, who takes over the company?"

"Right now, his son, Thomas."

Tori and Bell looked at each other. His wording had caught their attention.

Tori, controlling her vampiric urges, whispered to Bell, "Abraham and I heard Thorne talking to him about a new will earlier."

Bell smiled and looked back at Cartwright. "I understand Mr. Thorne asked you to draw up a new will."

"I'm afraid I can't discuss that matter."

"This is a murder investigation, Mr. Cartwright," Bell said. "Regardless of attorney-client privilege, we need to uncover suspects with a strong motive. Now, what did Mr. Thorne want you to do in this new will?"

Cartwright took a deep breath. "He wanted to disinherit

the children."

"Why?"

"He was displeased with the choices they made in their lives."

"Like what?" Bell asked.

"I can't say. I am their lawyer."

"Alright," Bell said, frustrated. "Then tell me about Julian Spade."

"He's a rival Egyptologist and very wealthy man," Cartwright replied.

"Did they get along?" Bell asked.

"They detested each other," Cartwright replied.

"Enough for Spade to want to kill Thorne?" Bell asked.

"Perhaps."

"And how did *you* get along with your client?" Bell asked.

"Very well."

"How long have you been the attorney for Thorne and his company?"

"Since before he was married to the children's mother, Sophia."

"What happened to her?" Bell asked.

"She died in a car accident with her first-born son, Gilbert, when the family vacationed in Italy before the war."

"So, Thomas was not Mr. Thorne's only son?" Tori asked.

"Gilbert was Sophia's son by her marriage to an American copper tycoon who died in 1901. Mr. Thorne married her in 1903."

"Did Thorne Industries take over the copper interests that used to belong to Mrs. Thorne's first husband?" Bell asked.

"She let him manage them with the understanding that Gilbert would take over when he completed his education and came of age. She retained legal control."

"I see," Bell replied, writing all this information down on his pad. "With Mr. Thorne gone, what will happen to you now?"

"I imagine his son, Thomas, will ask me to remain as lead counsel and advisor."

"The power behind the throne," Tori said.

Bell gave Tori a stern look and decided that Abraham already owed him a favor.

"What are you implying, young lady?" Cartwright asked.

"I'm implying that you will probably be a powerful influence on the new head of Thorne Industries," Tori said, putting on a look of innocence. "Is that inaccurate?"

Cartwright remained silent.

"With the new will Mr. Thorne asked you to draw up, who would have taken over his company?"

"That would have been me."

Tori and Bell glanced at each other again. Cartwright had no reason to kill Thorne before he signed the new will.

"Is there anything you would like to add, Mr. Cartwright?" Bell asked.

"I don't believe so. May I ask if I can remain when you interview Agatha and Thomas?"

Before Bell could answer, the door to the room opened, and Police Chief Bridges walked in. He saw Bell and motioned for him to come over to the corner of the room to brief him on the progress of the investigation so far. While the two men conversed, Tori could sense the insecurity surrounding Cartwright. *He's hiding something,* she thought. *But what is it?* She turned her attention to Bell and Bridges. The police chief was asking Bell about her.

"Who is she?"

"She's an associate of Mueller," Bell replied. "He said he would call you and explain."

"Okay, leave that for now. Just do what I told you about the guests and report to me in the morning."

"Yes, sir. Have a good rest of the evening."

Bridges left the room. Bell returned to the table and told his two officers to gather the addresses and phone numbers of all the guests outside the principal persons of interest.

"Mr. Cartwright, please tell the children, Mr. Grantham, and Colin that they can go home, and we will join them in a little while to question them."

"I will, detective. Thank you."

"Where are you all staying?"

"At the new Normandie."

"Good," Bell said. "Tell them we'll meet with them soon."

Cartwright left the room.

"What was that with Bridges?" Tori asked.

"Some of the guests called the mayor and complained that we were needlessly detaining them. I had to let everyone go."

"What about Spade?" Tori asked.

"We'll get to him after we talk with the rest of the family," Bell said. "What did you think of Cartwright?"

"I think he's hiding something."

"Not surprising. People in his position usually are. Let's find out if it has any bearing on this case. Let's speak to Sommers before we go. Remember, I still take the lead on the questions."

"Naturally," Tori replied with a wide grin.

Chapter Ten

October 15, 1928
Los Angeles Morgue/Coroner's Office
10:30 p.m.

In the medical examiner's room, Morris and Mueller examined both bodies and found no obvious fatal wounds other than the two broken necks. They also looked for any markings or evidence that the linen was used to commit the crime.

"So, both men expired by one or more persons of the non-mummy variety breaking their necks," Morris said.

"Let's not be totally dismissive of the mummy theory just yet."

"Oh, not again, Abraham," Morris said, exasperated. "Someone dropped the linen by the bodies and the exhibit to throw us off. They probably just ripped these pieces off the mummy and placed them on the floor."

"Very probably," Abraham replied. "I just think we should consider all possibilities for now. I think for the public, we should tell them it was a person or persons shifting blame to the mummy's curse. Remember how we handled the vampire killings last year?"

"I do, but what are the odds of us landing two supernatural murders in a little more than a year?"

"I admit the odds are against that, Scott."

The morgue orderly entered the room. "Excuse me, Dr. Morris. The police are bringing another body. He was found not far from the museum. He, uh, doesn't look too good."

The orderly returned a couple of minutes later with the new arrival. Morris pulled the sheet off the body, and both he and Abraham were aghast. It was a middle-aged, heavy-set male who had received multiple stab wounds to the torso and whose face had been mutilated. He was wearing a dinner suit.

"It won't be hard to figure out the cause of death here," Abraham said.

"Look what they did to his face," Morris said, still horrified. "What torture they inflicted on him. From the blood all over the face, they did that to him before they killed him."

"This looks like it was personal," Abraham said.

"Do you think this is Thorne's other bodyguard?"

"Could be," Abraham replied. "He's wearing a suit, but that doesn't mean anything. He could be from another party or event. What they did to the face makes identification challenging."

They began examining the body, starting with the head, and noticed a large bulge in his trachea.

"Hand me a scalpel," Morris said to the orderly.

After receiving it, he made an incision over the bulge and put his finger through the wound. "We have something hard here. Hand me the forceps."

A moment later, he pulled out a blue, oval object.

"Well," Abraham said, staring at the object. "We can safely say that this is Thorne's bodyguard."

"How?" Morris asked.

"You're holding what looks like the Eye of Aten."

"You sure?"

Abraham, remembering when he last saw the impressive ancient object several millennia before, said, "Pretty sure. Have the orderly take some pictures."

"Why would they shove it down his throat?" Morris asked.

"Good question," Abraham replied, taking hold of the Eye, examining it, and then smiling. "Let me call Bell."

CHAPTER ELEVEN

Normandie Hotel
605 South Normandie Avenue
Los Angeles, California
10:45 p.m.

U pon entering the opulent, Art Deco furnished Thorne suite at the Normandie Hotel, Tori thought to herself, *The rich and shameless in 1928 L.A.*

Thomas led the group to the living room, where everyone, except Tori and Bell, sat down. Among the attendees were Agatha, Ava, Thomas, Cartwright, Grantham, Sommers, Spade, Sullivan, Colin, and two police officers. Hanging over the fireplace was a portrait of a blonde woman embracing a teenage boy.

"Who's that?" Ava asked Agatha.

"My mother, Sophia, and my brother, Gilbert," Agatha said, staring fondly at the painting. "The artist completed the portrait in Italy days before they died."

"I'm sorry," Ava said, putting her hand on Agatha's shoulder.

"Thank you," she said, giving Ava a smile. "Colin, please see if anyone would like a drink."

"Very good, Miss Agatha," Colin replied.

As Colin went around the room, Bell began the conversation.

"Mr. Cartwright," he said. "Can you get us those documents you mentioned to us earlier? We want to review them."

"Very well," Cartwright said, rising from his seat and entering Mr. Thorne's office.

Bell took a moment to look at each face in the room. "Thank you all for coming this evening. I know it's been long and trying, but we'll try to get you out of here as soon as possible. Let's see. Where can we do the interviews?"

"The office that Cartwright went into should work," Tori suggested.

"Good idea," Bell replied.

"Can you speak with me first?" Sullivan asked. "With the passing of Mr. Thorne, I have to prepare for an entirely new broadcast."

"Sure," Bell replied. "We'll just wait for Cartwright to come—"

A loud explosion rocked the room. It seemed to come from Thorne's office, where Cartwright had been.

"BLAKE," Thomas roared, springing to his feet and running to the office.

Tori and Bell ran after him with the rest of the group in tow. Bell practically ran into Thomas, who had stopped in the doorway. The safe door had been blown open, and what was left of Cartwright lay on the floor under the desk.

Tori was initially overwhelmed by the sight and smell of the blood plastered across the walls, windows, and carpets. She had to step out and compose herself for a moment.

"Everyone back to the living room," Bell said, signaling an officer. "Nobody but us goes near the body."

Bell noticed that Tori looked a little pale. "Are you going

to be okay?"

Tori thought for a moment, trying to regain her self-control. *You can do this,* she told herself, as she took a couple of deep breathes. She refocused and looked at Bell. "I'll be alright."

"Would you like a handkerchief to mask the smell?" Bell asked, reaching into his jacket.

"I'll be fine," Tori replied, thinking the handkerchief would do little to dampen her enhanced senses.

Bell and Tori walked into the office, careful not to step on anything. Pieces of Cartwright's face were scattered across the room.

"I think I see one of his eyes by the window," Tori whispered to Bell.

"Come on," Bell whispered back. "Let's be sensitive about this."

"You're right," Tori replied. "I guess the one good thing is we can cross him off the suspect list."

Bell gave her another look then turned to the remaining officer. "Call the coroner's office. Morris has more business tonight. Get pictures of all this, too."

Bell pulled a pair of gloves from his breast pocket, put them on, and examined the safe. There was some burnt wiring attached to the interior of the door. He motioned Tori to come over. "Look here. It was wired to the explosive, and it triggered when Cartwright opened the safe."

"Ouch," Tori said, grimacing.

Mueller, Morris, and the orderly arrived a half hour later.

"Just before you called," Abraham said to Bell, "I told Scott we had to call you."

"You boys are keeping me busy," Morris said, glancing at the office. "I haven't had this much excitement in a long time. Is it okay to take him after I make my examination and note the observations?"

Bell nodded.

"Don't forget to pick up the parts scattered across the

room," Tori said.

Bell sighed, and Abraham shot Tori a nasty look, signaling to her to cut out the sarcastic remarks.

As Morris and the orderly were wheeling the remains of Cartwright out, Richardson entered the room.

Bell's face flushed red, and he moved to stand between Richardson and the rest of the suite. "How the hell did you get in here?"

"I never reveal my sources," Richardson replied, grinning.

"He probably tipped the bellboy," Tori said.

Richardson's face fell.

Bell turned to one of his officers. "Get him out of here, even if you have to carry him. And tell that bellboy we'll bring him in if he lets any other unauthorized individuals up here."

"Wait," Richardson pleaded. "It'll help me get a more accurate take on the story."

"No way," Bell said. He took a deep breath and pinched the bridge of his nose. "Please get him out of here."

"Sir," the officer said, gesturing to the door. "I'd hate to have to pick you up."

Without making more of a fuss, Richardson walked out with the police officer.

"Bring Thomas Thorne in here," Bell ordered one of the officers. A moment later, the new head of Thorne industries entered the room accompanied by Agatha, Ava, Colin, Spade, and Grantham.

"Mr. Thorne," Bell said to Thomas. "These items were in the safe." Bell placed the items, each one in a clear, plastic bag, on the table. "To your knowledge, was there anything else in the safe?"

Thomas looked at each item then frowned. "The money seems to be gone."

"How much was there?" Bell asked.

"I think five thousand. My father always kept extra cash for emergencies."

"Was there anything else that could have been taken besides the money?" Bell asked.

"The burnt scraps of his will are here. There are also burnt fragments of incorporation papers for something called The Utopia Institute in Arizona."

"What is The Utopia Institute?" Bell asked.

"I have no idea," Thomas replied. "Agatha? Colin?"

"Never heard of it," Agatha said. "But father never involved me in the business. Colin?"

"I've never been there, Miss Agatha," Colin replied. "I stayed at the hotel in Tucson while your father visited the institute. I have no idea what it is."

"Anything else you can tell us about these items?"

"Nothing I can identify," Thomas replied.

"So," Tori said. "Everyone is sure it was just money that was taken."

Before anyone could reply, Abraham cut in. "I have an idea," he said, tossing the Eye of Aten at Spade, who caught it.

"The Eye of Aten!" Grantham said, incredulous. "You found it."

"Where was it?" Sommers asked.

"Lodged in the throat of the bodyguard, Cain."

"Wait, Cain was murdered?" Thomas said.

"Yes," Abraham replied. A dark look flashed across his face. "Rather brutally, I might add."

"There is a God," Grantham mumbled.

"Why would the murderer shove the Eye of Aten down his throat?" Agatha asked.

"Excellent question," Abraham replied, putting on his lecturing persona. "Mr. Spade and Mr. Grantham, would you please look at the Eye and respond to the young lady's question?"

Both Spade and Grantham examined the Eye as best as they

could. They looked at each other and nodded. Grantham spoke first, "It's a fake."

"A fake," Sommers repeated, knitting his brow. "Thorne was going to display a fake in my museum? What a… Hold on. Then where's the real Eye?"

"I suspect," Bell said, "that up until a little while ago, it was in that safe. After dispatching Cain and giving him the fake eye as a last meal, the perp must have broken in here and stolen the real artifact."

"But how would they know where to look?" Tori asked. "Who would have known it was here?"

"If the thief had confederates on the inside, they would have told them where to look," Abraham said.

"Wait a second," Thomas said. "Are you treating *us* as suspects in this case?"

He's a dim one, Tori thought to herself.

"For now, everyone who was at the reception when the lights went off is considered a suspect," Bell said. He looked at Sullivan, who hadn't said a word since the explosion. "I don't care if the person is a professed Man of God or a person of means or a grieving child of the victim. Everyone is under consideration."

"This is ludicrous," Agatha said, crossing her arms. "Why would Thomas and I want to kill our own father?"

"Before we go there," Bell said, turning his attention back to Reverend Sullivan. "I was about to interview the Reverend. Where else can we go to do this with just him? This room won't do anymore."

"The bedroom has three chairs and a desk, sir," Colin said.

"Thank you, Colin," Bell replied. He looked at the Thorne family and entourage members. "My officers will make sure you're comfortable. Do not leave this room."

Tori, Bell, Mueller, and Sullivan followed Colin to the bedroom and set up the chairs and desk as an interview station.

"Thank you, Colin," Bell said. "Please tell the others that we'll ask for them soon."

"Very good, sir."

"Please sit down, Reverend."

Sullivan sat on one side of the desk while Tori and Bell sat on the other side. Mueller stood behind them.

Bell passed Tori his pencil and notepad.

"Can you please take notes for me, Miss Jacobsen?"

"Of course," Tori replied, a little upset that Bell assigned her the secretarial job. *These are the times,* she thought to herself.

"What was the broadcast with Mr. Thorne going to be about?" Bell asked.

"Our concerns about the Herbert Hoover presidential candidacy and what he will do to the country if he's elected."

Tori snickered, thinking, *He's right but for the wrong reasons.*

Sullivan glared at Tori. "At least he's not the Pope's candidate, Al Smith."

"What else were you going to discuss?"

"We were going to discuss enlarging our movement of White Christian Nationalism across the country."

God, Tori thought, *I hope this bastard dies next.*

"To what end?" Bell asked.

"To possibly consider a run for the Presidency in 1932 in the likely scenario that Mr. Hoover charts too progressive and inclusive a course for the country."

"Alright," Bell said, glancing at the notes Tori was taking. "Where were you when the lights went out, Reverend?"

"I was with Mr. Cartwright finalizing the scope of Mr. Thorne's appearance on my radio show."

"Mr. Cartwright did tell us that earlier," Tori said.

"You can go, Reverend," Bell said, "but we'll keep in touch."

"Thank you," Sullivan replied.

Bell asked Tori to go get Agatha. As she followed Sullivan, she saw him engage in conversation with the Thorne children.

"Your father was a great man of vision," Sullivan said, walking over to Agatha and Thomas. "My door is open, if you would like to discuss continuing it."

"We don't think so," Thomas said. "My sister and I have a different world view than my father or Mr. Cartwright. We'll be taking Thorne Industries in a more *enlightened* direction."

Sullivan smirked at Thorne's children and left.

"What an asshole," Ava said. "I'll be so happy when you and Thomas take him off the payroll."

"Totally," Agatha agreed. "I won't miss him."

"Detective Bell would like to speak with you, Miss Thorne."

Agatha followed Tori into the bedroom and took the seat that Sullivan had occupied.

"Now, Detective Bell," Agatha said. "Why would my brother and I want to kill my father?"

"Mr. Cartwright told us your father was going to disinherit you."

"Again?" Agatha said, unsurprised. "Our father was always threatening that. You can ask Colin or anyone else who lived or associated with us."

"But this time it was for real," Bell said. "Cartwright had drawn up a new will that would have cut both of you off. All it needed was your father's signature. Mr. Thorne was also going to fire Grantham from future archeological projects."

"So?" Agatha replied.

"We understand that you and he are involved," Bell said.

"That's true, but we would never kill my father. Why would we let him ruin our lives from the great beyond?"

"He also had you arrested at the Women's Rights Rally and thrown in jail with your friends," Abraham added.

"I still wouldn't have killed him over that," Agatha said, tearing up. "Even though I hated him, he was still my father."

"Where were you when the lights went off, Ms. Thorne?" Bell asked.

"I was with Ava and Trevor by the hors d'oeuvres table."

"Did you see anyone enter the room where your father and the bodyguard were found?"

"No, I was not paying attention."

"Okay. Thank you. Ms. Jacobsen, can you get Miss Perez and Mr. Grantham? Please make sure they don't say anything to each other."

"Yes, Detective Bell," Tori replied.

A few minutes later, Miss Perez and Mr. Grantham entered the room. Trevor let Ava have the seat.

"Where were you two when the lights went out?" Bell asked.

"The three of us were by the hors d'oeuvres table," Grantham replied.

Ava nodded in agreement.

"Did any of you see anyone go into the room the bodies of Mr. Thorne and the bodyguard were found in?"

Both shook their heads.

"Mr. Grantham," Bell said. "I understand that Mr. Thorne was about to dismiss you."

"So, what?" Grantham said. "I've already agreed to join Mr. Spade's team."

"We'll follow up with him. Miss Perez, how did you know Mr. Thorne?"

"I only met him this evening."

"But he had you arrested along with his daughter at the Woman's Right's Rally and thrown into jail," Tori said.

"That's true."

"That might be considered a motive," Bell said.

"It might be, but I didn't do it," Ava replied. "I have two

witnesses that can confirm it."

"Two witnesses who also have motives," Abraham said.

Ava and Trevor said nothing.

"Miss Jacobsen, please take them back and bring in Sommers and Spade."

"Yes, Detective," Tori replied.

Bell looked at Abraham and sighed. "Are they all going to provide alibis for each other?"

"Looks that way," Abraham said. "Unfortunately, I'm an alibi for Spade. I was talking with him when the lights went out."

"Doesn't mean he didn't hire killers to do the work for him."

Sommers and Spade followed Tori into the room. Sommers sat down while Spade stood by Mueller.

"Mr. Spade," Bell said. "I understand you just hired Mr. Grantham to be a project leader on your archeological digs."

"Yes, we agreed to the terms yesterday."

"Why were you in attendance at the museum tonight, Mr. Spade?" Bell asked. "I thought Thorne hated you."

"I can answer that," Sommers replied. "I invited him to speak as a guest panelist this evening."

"You invited a person Thorne loathed to an event celebrating his discovery?" Bell asked.

"I thought Mr. Thorne would handle it better," Sommers said.

"Did Thorne voice his displeasure to you?" Tori asked. "I saw him speaking with you before the lights went off."

Sommers gave Tori a "crap, caught" look. "Yes, he did."

"Out with it, man," Bell said. "We'll find out sooner or later."

"He was going to cut off a major donation to the museum because I invited Mr. Spade."

"Sounds like another person with a possible motive," Abraham muttered.

"Don't worry, Mr. Sommers," Spade said. "If you didn't kill

Thorne, I'll match the donation he withdrew."

"Bless you, sir."

"And where were you at the time of the murder, Mr. Sommers?"

"He was actually talking with me," Spade said, answering for Sommers.

Abraham gave Spade a quizzical stare.

"Really?" Bell said. "Professor Mueller said you were with him, Mr. Spade."

"Yes, but that was just before the lights went out. I bumped into Professor Sommers when I came back into the reception room."

Bell looked at Abraham, who nodded. "Yes, it could have happened that way."

"Alright," Bell said. "Did either of you see anyone go into the room that the bodies were found in?"

"I didn't," Spade said.

"Me either," Sommers replied. "There was a lot of confusion."

"Okay," Bell said, turning toward Tori, who was writing everything down. "Miss Jacobsen."

"Thomas now?"

"You read my mind."

"Come with me, gentlemen," Tori said, leading Sommers and Spade to the main room.

Bell smiled. "For a moment there, I thought we had our first crack in the questioning."

Tori entered with Thomas and Agatha.

"Miss Thorne," Bell said. "We need to speak to your brother alone."

"Please, Detective Bell," Agatha pleaded. "This is very difficult for my brother. He needs me here for support. I promise I won't make trouble."

Bell looked at Tori and Abraham. They were both confident that they'd detect any ulterior motives Agatha had and gestured for Bell to carry on.

"Alright," Bell said, shifting his attention to Thomas. "Mr. Thorne, I understand that you also have a motive for doing your father in."

Thomas looked at Agatha. "Yes, I probably have the biggest motive to kill my father." He covered his face and started to cry.

Agatha went to comfort him.

"I'm sorry if I am causing you pain, Thomas," Bell said. "But can you explain how you had the biggest motive?"

Thomas roared, "BECAUSE THE WOMAN I LOVED COMMITTED SUICIDE AFTER MY FATHER BLACKMAILED HER."

"How did he blackmail her?" Abraham asked.

"The son of a bitch knew about a relationship she had with someone else before me. He raped her. She became pregnant and had an abortion. My father threatened to ruin her and her family."

"Her having an abortion did not trouble you?" Tori asked, looking up from her notes.

"Of course not," Thomas said, looking confused. "She was a victim, though my father didn't seem to care."

"Was that the only reason your father was opposed to the two of you dating?" Bell asked.

"He thought she was beneath me because she did not come from the upper class."

"I see," Bell replied. "How did she die?"

"She poisoned herself about a month ago."

"My condolences," Abraham said, feeling for the boy. "Where were you when the lights went out, Thomas?"

"I was with Colin. He was trying to comfort me after I got into an argument with Dad."

"Did you see anyone enter the room where the bodies were found?" Bell asked.

Thomas shook his head.

"Miss Thorne, you can take your brother to the other room. Miss Jacobsen, please get Colin."

A few minutes later, Tori brought Colin in. Bell motioned for the butler to sit but he declined, preferring to stand.

"How long have you been Mr. Thorne's butler, Colin?" Bell asked.

"Since just before his marriage to the children's mother."

"So, you've known him as long as the newly-departed Mr. Cartwright?" Tori asked.

"That's correct, miss."

"How did you get on with him?" Bell asked.

"I don't wish to speak ill of the dead, sir, and it's not my place."

"So, you hated him, too?" Abraham asked.

Colin did not respond.

"I'll take that as a yes," Bell said, glancing at Tori. "Where were you at the time of the blackout?"

"I was consoling Thomas after he got into an argument with his father."

"Over his recently deceased girlfriend?" Abraham asked.

"Yes, sir. She was the love of his life."

"Did you know her, Colin?" Tori asked.

"Yes, Miss Jacobsen, I did." Colin shook his head. "It was obscene what Mr. Thorne put her and Master Thomas through."

"It seems like Mr. Thorne was capable of a lot of obscene behavior," Abraham said.

"He was," Colin replied. "May I go now, Detective?"

"One last question. During the blackout, did you see anyone enter the room where the bodies were discovered?"

"No, sir."

"Okay, Colin," Bell said. "You may go."

Bell turned to Tori and Abraham. "Damn. They all have alibis."

"That's a nuisance," Tori said, flipping through her notes.

"What should we do with them?" Bell asked. "I can't detain all of them. The chief got raked over the coals when all the guests complained about being detained at the museum reception. And with them all having alibis, I've got nothing to hold them on until we dig deeper."

"Let them go," Tori said. "You're right when you say we don't have anything strong enough to make an arrest. Let's go back to Mueller's place and start to piece this together. That way, we won't have the chief hovering over us."

"Good idea," Bell said. "You know, she would be a good addition to the force, Abraham, if she wasn't—"

"A woman?" Tori interrupted.

"A wise ass," Bell replied.

"I agree," Abraham said, smiling. "She'd be an asset here if she learned to keep her mouth shut."

"Thank you, gentlemen," Tori said, grinning.

Bell smiled and led the others to the main room with the suspects. "I think I have everything I need for now. We're going to lock the office up. No one is to go in there. Do not leave Los Angeles. We will want to follow up with all of you. Have a good evening."

As Tori, Abraham, and Carl were leaving, Spade pulled Abraham aside. "We must talk. The Eye is out there, and we must find it."

"I know. I'll call you later. Give me your number and address."

Spade wrote his phone number and address on a piece of scrap paper and gave it to his old acquaintance.

"Good. I'll call you soon."

Abraham whispered to Tori, "What can you sense?"

"Unfortunately, everyone, including the now-deceased Cartwright, is hiding something. I think the best way to crack this case is see who is left standing after all the intended victims are killed."

"Cut the sarcasm. Let's see if we can solve it without a high mortality rate," Abraham said.

CHAPTER TWELVE

The men who helped kill Thorne and the two bodyguards moved the mummy of Sennefer into an isolated room at an abandoned warehouse just outside of Los Angeles.

"Do we meet the boss at the hotel, Ernie?"

"No, Justin. He said to meet him here."

"That's right," a tall, Middle Eastern man said, entering the room. He saw the coffin and inspected the mummy. "Good job bringing it here."

"Were you able to get the Eye?" Ernie asked.

The man took the blue, oval crystal out of his pocket and tossed it up and down a few times.

"Then our job is done?" Justin asked.

"Yes," the man said. "You've done well helping me get revenge on Thorne and Cain."

"We're glad, Mr. Andoheb," Ernie said. "I guess it's time to settle up."

"You're right, gentlemen," Andoheb said, pulling out a revolver. "For your invaluable service."

Before they could react, Andoheb shot each man through the head. "That was cheaper than paying in dollars."

Offices of the Los Angeles Herald
Just after 2:00 a.m.

Richardson was pleased with the headline he created for the upcoming morning edition: "Mummy's Vengeance Strikes at Natural History Museum."

So was his editor, Barry Black, who patted Richardson on the back for the outstanding narrative he composed reporting on the murder.

"I don't know if it will get me a Pulitzer, but it sure will bring in more readers."

"That headline sure will," Black said.

"The mayor and the police chief might get on us, thinking the headline and story will cause a panic with our telling of the mummy's vengeance."

"So, what?" Black said. "Our job is to grow and engage our readership. Their job is to solve the crime as fast as possible, so there is no panic."

"Yes, sir."

Richardson's phone rang. It was one of his informants at the police station.

"They're at Mueller's house," Richardson said to Black. "Thank you… What's that? Yeah, I know where he lives. Thank you again."

CHAPTER THIRTEEN

October 16, 1928
About 3:00 a.m.
Professor Abraham Mueller's house, outside Los Angeles

In the living room, Abraham set up an easel board with a large pad of paper, so he, Tori, and Bell could work on the mystery at hand. Frank served everyone some sandwiches and water. While he prepared the refreshments, Tori changed out of her dress into a women's travel suit.

"This sandwich is pretty good," Bell said. "Your butler knows how to cook."

"I'll be sure and let him know you're happy," Tori said.

"Okay," Abraham said. "Let's see where we are. Who do we see as the prime suspects?"

"Definitely the people we interviewed in the hotel room," Bell replied. "They all had motives to kill Thorne. The bodyguards were just in the way."

"If Cain died the way the other bodyguard did," Abraham said, uncapping a marker, "I would agree. But someone went to a great deal of trouble to butcher him."

"Do you think he was the intended target?" Tori asked.

"I don't think so," Abraham replied. "I think the murderer may be someone who felt wronged by both Thorne and Cain."

"From what I understand," Bell said, "Thorne used Cain as his enforcer, the one to do his dirty work while Thorne kept his hands clean."

"You would think that would greatly expand the list of suspects," Tori said.

"Perhaps," Bell replied. "But my money is still on someone in that hotel room. Maybe they had an eager accomplice who had the same axe to grind with the victims."

"That makes sense," Abraham said. "If they needed an alibi to stay in the reception room when the lights went out, they would have their confederate do the jobs for them."

"If a confederate was even involved," Tori said. "So that would leave Sommers out. He just found out about Thorne cutting off the funding last night. No time to search for a hired gun."

"If it went down that way," Bell said.

Abraham started to write the list of the names of the people in the hotel room. He then wrote the possible motives for each one except for Sullivan and Colin.

"I have to admit, I can't think of motives for Sullivan and Colin."

"Maybe the butler was a disgruntled employee," Tori said.

Both men laughed.

"Then again," Tori said, "he seemed pretty devoted to the children. There may be more there than meets the eye."

"I agree," Bell said. "I can't think of a motive for Sullivan to kill Thorne. They seemed like kindred spirits politically."

"I would suggest digging a little more," Abraham said, staring at the list of names. "There may be more below the surface on both. Looking at the list, I would give the son the best motive: the death of the woman he loved."

Bell nodded. "We should check up on who that poor woman was. My next suspect would be the daughter. Ambition and greed are the most powerful motives, and with the resources of Thorne industries, she could make significant advances in the fight for women's equal rights."

"And the daughter had a friend with her who might have gladly helped," Abraham said.

"I don't think so," Tori said. "Perez doesn't have the strength or size to take on that bodyguard. It could still be Grantham and Spade. A resentful employee and rival who both detested Thorne. Plus, Grantham is in love with Agatha. He probably didn't like how Thorne let her sit in jail for participating in that protest."

"Good point," Abraham said. "Spade would definitely have the means to recruit outside help."

"So would the brother and sister," Bell countered, "knowing they would be coming into a fortune. They could pay someone a retainer and take care of the rest after they inherit."

"But Spade has an added incentive," Tori said, glancing at Abraham. "The Eye of Aten."

"How valuable is that jewel?" Bell asked.

"Priceless in both value and purpose," Abraham said.

"What purpose?" Bell asked, frowning.

"According to legend, when combined with the Prayer of Aten, it could give the possessor the power to fulfill his or her wishes," Abraham said.

"You don't believe any of that crap, do you?" Bell asked.

"Of course not," Abraham lied.

"But if the murderer or person who ordered the murder believed it…" Tori said, trailing off.

"That would be a great motive," Bell said, completing the thought.

Outside, Richardson drove up the street and parked across from the house. It was the only house in the vicinity. He saw the lights still on and thought it was safe to go and knock on the door. As he approached, he saw a man crouched by the house.

"Hey!" Richardson shouted. "What are you doing over there?"

The man started and turned to face Richardson. It was Andoheb.

"Who the hell are you?" Richardson asked.

Without answering, Andoheb pulled out his revolver and fired. Richardson dove to the ground then scrambled to get behind his car. Andoheb, not having any time to take care of Richardson, ran down the street to his car. Richardson poked his head out from behind his car in time to see Andoheb drive away. He started to run towards Abraham's house when the spot by the front door exploded. Andoheb had planted a stick of dynamite by the part of the house where the living room was located.

"My God," Richardson said, rushing to the now burning house. He froze when he saw Tori, Abraham, and a hulking figure carrying Bell emerge from the flames. He couldn't understand how Bell was the only one who seemed to be injured.

"Holy shit," Richardson muttered.

Tori's eyes glowed, and her canine teeth protruded. "Which way did he go?"

Not able to say a word, Richardson pointed.

"Frank," Abraham said, as he started to transform into a wolf. "Take care of both of them and put the fire out."

"Yes, Master Abraham."

Abraham nodded to Tori, and she took off, flying to intercept Andoheb's car. Fully transformed into a wolf, Abraham followed.

"Holy Shit," Richardson repeated, thinking he was going to get in his car, follow them, and take the pictures that would definitely get him that coveted Pulitzer.

Frank gently placed Bell on the ground and put one of his enormous hands on Richardson's shoulders. "You stay."

Frightened at the prospect of tangling with Frank, Richardson nodded. "Whatever you say, big guy."

Andoheb sped down the dark, isolated road, hoping to avoid running into anyone else. He jumped when something landed on the roof of his car, and was horrified when it tore his car open like it was a can of tuna.

Tori, in full vampiric form, stared down at him. "Good evening." She pulled him out of the car, as he swerved off the road. Tori carried Andoheb with her and landed on the sidewalk, pinning him to the ground and clutching his neck.

By that point, Abraham caught up and stood by menacingly.

"It looks like I am going to have a good meal tonight after all."

"No, please don't," Andoheb said, squirming. "I'll tell you anything."

"Who are you, then?" Tori asked.

Too frightened not to respond, Andoheb told them who he was and why he killed Thorne, Cain, and the other bodyguard.

"Why did you mutilate Cain the way you did?"

"He killed and mutilated my brother."

Tori then asked, "Why kill us?"

"That's what my employer wanted."

"Who hired you?" Tori asked.

Andoheb hesitated.

Tori tightened her grip around his neck. "Did you forget I said you were the main course? WHO HIRED YOU?"

"SPADE," Andoheb, choking, shouted out. "IT WAS SPADE."

Tori looked at Abraham, who transformed back into his human form. He looked stunned and saddened.

Chapter Fourteen

October 16, 1928
About 3:00 a.m.
Professor Abraham Mueller's house, outside Los Angeles

Richardson, sitting on the road next to his car, did not know what to make of Frank, who held Bell like he was a baby. They had quietly and diligently worked together to put out the fire.

"You guys are lucky the fire didn't spread to the rest of the house," Richardson said, wondering if there were rules or limits to Frank's speaking abilities.

Frank said nothing.

"How is Detective Bell?"

Frank looked down at Bell and placed his hand over his heart. He looked at Richardson and smiled. "He will live, but he is weak. He will need a doctor."

"I'm glad he's going to be okay," Richardson said, trying to slide over to his card door.

"Do not move," Frank said.

"Can't I just get my camera?"

"Not until the Master and Mistress say so."

"You keep saying Master and Mistress," Richardson said. "How can Mueller afford you as a butler?"

Frank did not respond.

"You *are* his butler, right?"

"I am their Golem servant."

"Golem?" Richardson frowned. "No way! I saw that German silent movie. I thought you were some sort of Jewish Fairy Tale."

Frank was silent again.

A moment later, Tori landed on the road next to Richardson's car, unceremoniously dumping Andoheb on the ground. He was bruised and unconscious but otherwise unharmed.

Richardson opened his mouth to speak, but Tori waved him off. "Quiet."

Abraham returned shortly after Tori. Richardson tried to speak again, but Abraham growled at him, muttering, "You heard the lady. Be quiet. Good job putting out the fire, Frank."

"The talkative one helped," Frank replied, looking at Richardson.

"How is Carl?" Tori asked.

"He'll live, but we need to get him to a doctor, Mistress."

"Okay," Abraham said, "we'll get him to the hospital. Frank, take our other guest to the cell in the basement and make sure he doesn't make trouble."

"Yes, Master."

"Hold on," Richardson interrupted.

Abraham growled again, and Tori's eyes turned bright red.

Richardson swallowed. "Uh, never mind. Lead the way, big guy."

Frank handed Bell over to Abraham and pulled Richardson up from the road. "Follow me."

Richardson followed Frank, muttering, "A mummy's curse

with a vampire, a werewolf, and a golem. Forget the Pulitzer. I can make millions with the movie rights. Maybe Lon Chaney can play *all* the roles. He's so good with the makeup."

Tori looked concerned while eying Richardson and Frank. "What are we going to do about him?"

"You'll hypnotize him later and make him forget everything."

"If I can. It's not like I've had a lot of practice with that."

"We'll cross that bridge when the time comes," Abraham said. "Let's get Carl to the hospital and take our unconscious friend here back to his employer."

"We're not just going to tell the police chief and have him arrest Spade?"

"No. They would be out of their element dealing with Spade. We have to handle this."

Chapter Fifteen

Agatha, Ava, Thomas, Grantham, and Sommers were still sitting in the living room of the Thorne suite. Colin had served them drinks, and they talked about their hopeful dreams for the future and how glad they were that Mr. Thorne was no longer on this Earth.

"Is it bad form to toast the murderer?" Grantham asked.

Everyone laughed.

"Maybe just a little," Thomas replied. "We *do* have to keep up some level of respect and decorum here, no matter how undeserved."

"It's a shame that Blake is gone," Agatha said.

"He would have been good to keep on for the transition," Grantham said.

"Maybe," Thomas replied. "He might have tried to control things from behind the scenes, and it could have gotten ugly with him. Still, he was able to stop dad from exercising his worst impulses, and, unlike him, he didn't deserve what happened to him."

"May I suggest, Master Thomas," Colin said, entering the room, "that you all retire? There will be much to do in the morning, and you all need some sleep."

"That's a good suggestion, Colin, and you're right. We are so indebted to you for your years of service to us. In many ways, you were more of a father to us than Mr. Thorne was."

"I relish the complement, Master Thorne."

"Before I forget!" Thomas said. "I looked through some of the papers on Dad's desk. There was some interesting correspondence between him and that zealot, Sullivan."

"Do you think it has anything to do with what happened last night?" Sommers asked.

"I'm not sure."

"We should probably turn that over to the police," Agatha said.

"Good idea," Thomas replied. "See to that later today, Colin."

"Yes, sir. I'll take it to the police station."

Ava rose from her seat and handed her glass to Colin. "Well. I guess it's bedtime for me. Call me tomorrow, Agatha, and we can start planning for the future."

The two ladies embraced.

After Ava left, Sommers rose from the couch and said goodbye to everyone. Thomas walked him out, patting him on the back. "I want you to know, John, that the museum will still receive the contribution dad promised before he had a fit."

Sommers happily shook Thomas's hand. "Thank you so much. The museum will be able to do a lot if you fulfill your father's commitment along with the promise Mr. Spade made."

"Safe travels home, sir."

After Sommers left, Thomas returned to the living room and found his sister getting chummy with Grantham. "Oh, come on you two. Just go to the bedroom."

"I'm sorry, Thomas," Grantham said.

"Don't be, Trevor," Agatha replied. "Thomas is just teasing us. He won't be like father."

"Heaven forbid. I hope you are both happy. I did just remember, Trevor. Is your deal with Spade formalized?"

"We're supposed to sign later today."

"Any chance you would reconsider and stay as our expedition leader?" Thomas asked.

"I gave my word to him on a two-year arrangement."

"I understand. Can you ask him if the agreement can commence in six months' time? That way, you can help us transition and find a new leader until we can lure you back in a couple of years."

"I can try."

"Good. Well, good night you two. Sweet dreams."

"You too, brother. Now we can make Thorne Industries something the people of the world can be proud of."

Colin checked on the couple one last time then retired to his chambers.

With the butler gone, Agatha gave Grantham a long kiss, which he reciprocated. "The rest of our lives are going to be so good now," she said.

"They will," Grantham replied. "No one will come between us now."

CHAPTER SIXTEEN

S pade was depressed. He hunched over his piano and played Beethoven's Moonlight Sonata, his eyes unfocused and his mind lost in the melody. He felt people enter the room through the window behind him but kept playing. He knew who they were.

Tori and the now-conscious Andoheb stayed by the window, and Abraham approached Spade.

"I thought you would be playing something more pleasant."

"It fits the situation we are now in," Spade replied. "Still, I always admired Ludwig for overcoming his deafness to produce such beauty and genius." He stopped and turned to Abraham. "You know, if you had just knocked, I would have answered the door. You didn't have to make a dramatic entrance with your vampire associate."

"We weren't sure how welcoming you would be," Tori said.

Spade turned and seemed startled by Andoheb.

"So you *do* know him," Abraham said.

"Of course, I do. He and his brother had dealings with me in Egypt."

"How about in the last 24 hours with Thorne and his bodyguards?" Tori asked.

"What are you talking about?"

"Andoheb, here, said you hired him to murder Thorne and the bodyguards, then steal the mummy and the Eye of Aten."

"And you *believed* him?" Spade said, looking hurt. "After all we've been through over the centuries?"

"I know you want the Eye," Abraham said. "After several thousand years, one might do *anything* to get what they want. Doesn't matter that he spent centuries redeeming himself and putting his checkered—shall we say formative? —years behind him." Abraham sighed. "We also know you and Thorne were unfriendly rivals."

"I don't have the Eye," Spade said. "And what's worse is I don't have the prayer of Aten either. Not anymore."

"What do you mean?" Tori asked.

"Look in my office over there."

Abraham motioned Tori to keep careful watch of both men, as he walked into Spade's office. Spade's butler was sprawled on the floor, dead. Above him was another empty, broken-into safe. No hieroglyph tablet with the Prayer of Aten. "Shit," he said. He stormed back into the living room.

"Tori, was Andoheb here under hypnosis when he told you Spade hired him?"

"No, he volunteered it."

"Hold on a minute," Spade said. "Is he the one responsible for the death of my servant?"

Andoheb started to sweat.

"Very probably," Abraham replied.

"Give me a minute with him," Spade said. "I remember some techniques from the Inquisition that should assist us here."

"While I appreciate the nostalgia of that, we have some cleaner options," Abraham said. "Tori, hypnotize him now."

Before Tori could pull Andoheb toward her, he bolted toward the open window, yelling "for my brother," and dove out. Tori rushed to the window and started to change, so she could fly, but it was too late. Andoheb was dead on the sidewalk.

"The question, now" Abraham said, "is did he die for you, old friend, or for someone else?"

"You really have to ask that question? You saw my butler. He served me faithfully for years. You saw the safe."

"Could be an attempt at misdirection," Abraham said. He smiled. "But probably not. Who was Andoheb *really* working for?"

"Someone he was really devoted to," Tori said.

"Who would that be from the current cast of suspects?" Abraham asked. "The Thorne children are more inclined toward helping people than their father."

"Grantham has a reputation as a caring expedition leader," Spade added.

"Then there's that Sullivan fanatic," Tori said. "I can see *him* inspiring both devotion and fear."

"He's the one," Abraham said, giving Tori a smile. "I can see him wanting the Eye and Prayer the most. He told us he and Thorne had political ambitions. What better way to achieve those than having those tools? The power that object has would be intoxicating even for someone who is a publicly-devout Christian leader."

"Let's call the police and inform them about my butler and Andoheb," Spade said. "Then we can pay Sullivan a visit."

"We?" Tori asked, giving Spade a look.

"Of course," Spade replied. "We all have a vested interest in getting the Eye and Prayer back."

"Like saving civilization?" Tori asked.

"I was thinking something more personal," Spade said.

"What's he talking about?" Tori asked, turning to Abraham.

"You haven't told her?" Spade's eyes went wide.

"I didn't want to get her hopes up."

"What hopes?" Tori asked, looking between the two ancient immortals.

Abraham turned to face Tori. "There's a chance the Eye coupled with the Prayer can cure us of our afflictions."

"That would be wonderful... if it's true," Tori said.

"Our sentiments exactly," Spade said. "Let's call the police and then pay a visit to the fake messiah."

"Do that," Abraham said, turning his attention to Tori. "Can you take a quick trip downstairs to check on Andoheb's clothing? We didn't search his pockets. He may have something."

"Understood," Tori replied.

Later, an overjoyed Bridges as good as skipped into the apartment. He was so happy that the murderer had been caught. "That saves me so much grief. Thank you all for your help."

"Well," Tori said. "Andoheb did all the work by jumping out the window."

"I'm very upset that my servant, Miles, is gone," Spade said quietly. "He was a good friend."

"Of course," Bridges said. "A terrible loss along with the other victims."

"Any leads on the stolen mummy and artifacts?" Abraham asked.

"None yet," Bridges said, "but we'll keep looking."

"Good," Abraham said. "How is Carl?"

"He has a concussion but should be out of the hospital in a couple days. We'll need you two to come to the office and give a report on what happened at your house."

"Of course," Abraham replied.

"Before I forget, have you seen that jackass Richardson?"

"Why do you ask, Chief?" Tori asked.

"Did you see the morning paper? That jerk put out a headline talking about the mummy's vengeance. I'll show those bastards at the Herald. I'll give the L.A. Times the scoop that the very mortal murderer has been caught. They'll look like sensationalist idiots."

"Sounds fair," Abraham said. "If we see Richardson, we'll let him know you are properly annoyed."

An officer came in and told them that the station had sent the Thorne butler over with some documents.

"We'll meet him outside," Bridges said.

Tori, Abraham, Spade, and Bridges met Colin outside the front door to the apartment. "Professor Mueller. Miss Jacobsen. The people at the station told me you were here."

"How can we help you, Colin?" Chief Bridges asked.

"Master Thomas thought you may want to look at these papers."

"What are they?" Abraham asked, taking them from Colin.

"Some correspondence between the late Mr. Thorne and Mr. Sullivan."

"No need to get into that can of worms," Bridges said, wiping his hands of the work. "The murderer has been caught."

"He has?" Colin asked. "May I ask who it is, so I can tell Mistress Agatha, Master Thomas, and the others?"

"Not yet," Bridges replied. "Maybe later this afternoon."

"Very good, sir. Good day, everyone."

"Good day, Colin," Spade said.

Colin walked out. Bridges followed shortly after, reminding Tori and Abraham to come to the station to fill out their reports. After everyone left, they poured over the correspondence between Thorne and Sullivan.

"So, we're not telling Bridges of our suspicions about Sullivan or the others?" Tori asked.

"Whatever for?" Abraham said. "Do you want them

sticking their noses in things they can't fathom? Better for us that they're out of it."

"It seems that Mr. Thorne had more of an appreciation for the Eye and the Prayer of Aten than I gave him credit for," Spade said, looking up from one of the letters. "He writes to Sullivan of knowing of ancient tools that could help them gain power in 1932 and keep it."

"Then," Tori said, "Andoheb could have been employed by Sullivan."

"It's a possibility," Abraham said. "What did you find on Andoheb?"

Tori pulled out a receipt to a warehouse on the outskirts of the city. "I think we may find our missing artifacts there."

"Let's get there quickly," Spade suggested. "We'll take my car."

"You two go ahead, and I'll catch up," Tori said. "I'll get Frank and Richardson."

"Richardson," Spade said, frowning. "What is he doing with you two?"

Tori shrugged. "He saw too much."

"Then do you think it's wise to bring him to the warehouse?" Spade asked.

"We can't let him write about what he saw," Abraham said.

"He'll be discredited in a couple hours after Bridges goes to the LA Times," Spade said. "Who's going to believe him after today?"

"He has a point," Tori said.

"Maybe," Abraham said. "Bring him anyway. I have a feeling it is better to be safe than sorry."

CHAPTER SEVENTEEN

October 16, 1928
Abandoned Warehouse

A braham and Spade pulled up to the warehouse in Spade's Rolls Royce Phantom. They parked next to a supply truck. "It's good to see the years have treated you well," Abraham said.

"Why not live well when you have the means?"

"I suppose that's one way to look at it," Abraham replied, observing the truck. "We kind of stick out though."

"Sorry about that. I know we're not exactly inconspicuous."

"There are probably people in there with the supply truck parked out here."

"Check my glove compartment," Spade said. "You'll find a trinket we can bring to the party."

Abraham opened the compartment and pulled out a colt revolver. "An original from last century."

"It helps to own a lot of shares in the company. You get special benefits."

"You'll never go broke investing in weapons."

"As our experiences through the millennia have taught us," Spade said. "Let's check the truck and see if anything has been packed."

The two men exited the car and looked over the truck. There was nothing in there. Abraham pointed to the path that led to the building entrance. "Well, let's go check inside."

As the centuries-old friends walked down to the front door, they found it was unlocked. Abraham turned the knob and slowly opened the door. They entered what was a lobby area and looked around. There was a staircase that led to a second floor and another path that led further down the ground level. They heard what sounded like two men talking to each other on the first floor. Abraham motioned Spade to be quiet, checked to make sure the colt was ready to fire, and led them down the hall where they heard the sound come from. They came upon a double door with glass windows at the top. They peeked in through the windows and saw two men putting the mummy of Sennefer, lying in his coffin, vertically on a dolly.

"So, you found the time to have him mummified?"

"Only the bandages," Abraham replied.

"Well, our old friend looks good," Spade whispered, seeing Sennefer for the first time since he killed him in the temple.

Their attention shifted when they saw two other men pull another large crate from another room. They could hear both of them complaining about how cold the contents of the box were.

"What the hell is *that*?" Abraham whispered.

"I don't know," Spade responded. "Could be another artifact, but I can't recall of any historically cold artifacts."

Abraham pulled Spade back, led him back to the front door, and whispered, "Let them take Sennefer and the other crate out and put them in the truck. You follow them, and I'll wait for the others."

"Then, what will you do?"

"Either meeting Sullivan or going to my office at the University. Leave a message with my secretary, Ida."

Chapter Eighteen

Tori and the others picked up Abraham at the warehouse. Frank started to drive them to Reverend Sullivan's office and radio station. While in the back seat of the car, Tori tried to hypnotize Richardson to make him forget what he saw at their house. Unfortunately, the journalist was not succumbing to Tori's attempts.

"It's not working, Abraham," Tori said.

"Maybe I just have a superior mind," Richardson said, giving Tori a grin.

Tori's eyes became red, her vampire teeth appeared, and her hands became claws as she gripped Richardson's neck. "Do you feel superior now, Mr. Richardson?"

"I suddenly… am at a loss for words," he choked out.

"Tori," Abraham said. "Let him go."

"Fine," she said, returning to her human form.

"Listen to me, William," Abraham said. "Right now, how do you see your options for being able to survive this drive if you don't cooperate with us?"

"Limited," Richardson said, massaging his throat.

"Bright lad. That headline of yours about the mummy's vengeance in the morning papers has upset the police chief and with his going to the LA Times with the identity of the non-supernatural murderer, by this evening, you will be the laughingstock of the city. How do you think your editor is going to feel about you, especially if you go to him with another outlandish story, without proof, of a vampire, a werewolf, and a golem in L.A.?"

"I think we can rule out getting a birthday card this year."

"In all likelihood, it'll be substituted with a severance notice," Tori interjected.

"Very probably," Abraham said. "But I know a way for you to get back in everyone's good graces and manage to live past today."

"I'm all ears."

"We think we know who's the brains behind the murders and the theft. If you help us, you'll get the scoop and be in line for that Pulitzer you're always salivating for."

"What about what I know about you three?"

"This is where it's decision time. If word ever gets out about our true natures," Abraham said at length, "you won't know it when the end comes. It could be a rabid dog devouring you when you're walking in a park. It could be someone breaking into your apartment, attacking you in your room, and biting you on the jugular. It could be a horrible driver not knowing you were in front of him."

"I'm getting better, Master Abraham."

"Yes, you are Frank. Keep watching the road. Well, do we have an understanding Mr. Richardson?"

The journalist looked at the three potential sources of his future demise and nodded. "It seems I have no choice."

"Excellent," Abraham said.

"Now, how can I help you?"

"I want you and Frank to go meet that Fascist maniac Reverend Sullivan and see if there is anything else you can find out about his relationship with Thorne other than what's in the correspondence Colin brought to us."

"I could use the pretext of following up about last night to see about talking with him," Richardson said. "What if he doesn't want to see me?"

"See what else you can find by observing what the people are doing in the office."

"What do we say our friend the Golem is?"

Tori picked up Richardson's camera. "He's your photographer."

"Can he take pictures?"

"What's your point?" Tori asked. "You just set it up for him and tell him what button to push. Frank's a quick learner."

"Thank you, Mistress Tori."

"He's also there to—"

"Make sure I don't run," Richardson said, completing Abraham's thought.

"He is quick, Abraham," Tori said.

"What are you guys going to be doing?"

"Waiting for you across the street in the car," Abraham replied.

Frank pulled up across the street from Sullivan's office and radio station.

"It's showtime," Tori said to Richardson. "Time to be a team player."

"Good luck," Abraham said. "Take good care of him, Frank."

"Yes, Master Abraham," Frank responded, taking the camera and holding it upside down. "We'll be fine."

Richardson gently took the camera from Frank, put it in the right position and handed it back to him.

"Thank you," the Golem said.

"Don't mention it."

Richardson and Frank got out of the car and walked across the street, entering Sullivan's office. Staffers were busy preparing for that evening's rally at the Hollywood Bowl. Frank picked up one of the flyers advertising the event.

"This could be important," Frank said, putting it in his pocket.

"Maybe," Richardson replied, going over to the secretary at the front desk. He identified himself and asked if Mr. Sullivan was available. She asked them to wait and left her desk to check with Sullivan in his office. After a moment, she returned and motioned them to go in.

Sullivan, with a confident grin, stood behind his desk and asked them to sit down. They sat down in the two chairs across from the radio personality. Sullivan appeared in awe at the sight of Frank.

"I must say, I'm surprised to see you, Mr. Richardson," Sullivan said, not taking his eyes off Frank. "I heard you weren't long for this city after your sensational headline story backfired on you."

"My editor is a forgiving man," Richardson said, trying to ignore the jab. "My photographer and I are here on a follow-up story on your relationship with Mr. Thorne. Would you like to discuss it?"

"I plan on giving a rousing tribute to my friend this evening at the rally at the Hollywood Bowl. If you're still employed by then, come by and hear what I have to say."

"But I understand he was going to be a guest on your radio show today."

"That's true."

"My sources said you were going to discuss the inadequacies of Secretary Hoover. Is that true?" Richardson asked.

"Come tonight and find out," the Reverend replied.

"Do you want to give me any advance copy before then?"

"No. Now if you'll excuse me. I'm very busy."

"One last thing if I may. When did you and Mr. Thorne meet?"

"In the late summer/early fall of 1920."

"Just as you were starting to gain popularity in the Great Lakes and Midwest."

"That's true," Sullivan replied.

"Was Thorne a patron?"

"You can say that. Now I really have to go. Good day."

Richardson nodded and motioned Frank to follow him out of Sullivan's office. When they left, Sullivan looked back at his bookshelf across from his desk. He pulled out a volume called *Jewish Folklore* and opened to the index. After scanning the G section, he found what he was looking for and went to the lobby area to watch Richardson and Frank go to their car. "A Golem," he muttered to himself.

After Frank and Richardson returned to the car, Abraham asked how it went. Richardson told them about the rally.

"I guess we're going to the Hollywood Bowl," Tori said.

CHAPTER NINETEEN

October 16, 1928
The Los Angeles Herald

Richardson's editor, Barry Black, was in no mood to listen to the young journalist's claims that he was onto something on the Thorne murder after the mayor and the police chief both called, threatening legal action for the morning release of the sensational story about the mummy's vengeance. What made matters worse was that the Los Angeles Times ran an exclusive, provided by the police chief, stating that the real, non-supernatural murderer had been found and killed.

"I don't want to hear it, Richardson," Black said, barely visible behind the clutter on his desk. "The thing I want you to do clean up your desk and get the hell out of here."

"But Barry—"

"Mr. Black, to you. Just get out of here and don't show your face again."

Tori, who accompanied Richardson to his editor's office, sat across from the desk and was halfway amused at William's predicament but also sorry because Black was clearly being a hypercritical ass.

"May I say something on William's behalf?" Tori asked, getting up from her seat.

"I'm sorry, who are you again?" Black asked.

"My name is Victoria Jacobsen, and I'm a friend of William's. I think you should give him another chance."

Impressed by Tori's figure, Black mellowed and asked, "Why should I do that?"

Tori came to the desk and sat on the edge right in front of Black, looking straight into his eyes. She spoke in a soothing tone. "Because he does have a potential scoop on the Thorne murder that would make front page news."

Black sat back in his chair, shaking his head. "I don't know."

"Look at me, Barry," Tori said.

The editor dutifully turned and faced Tori.

She continued in a calming tone. "Give him this chance."

"But the owners of the paper want him gone."

"Don't tell them you're giving him this chance. If he messes up, you're a hero for firing him. If he brings you a scoop, you're a hero for sticking your neck out for him, and the paper makes lots of money. Your owners will like that."

Black tried to take his eyes off Tori's face, but he could not resist.

"Come on, Barry," Tori said. "Just one more chance. What have you got to lose?"

"Alright," Black replied. "He has 24 hours and not one minute more."

"Thank you," Tori said, offering her hand. "You've been very helpful."

Black shook Tori's hand. "My pleasure. Perhaps later, we can meet for a drink."

"I'm afraid not," Tori replied. "I don't drink alcohol. Thank you again."

Tori led Richardson out of the office.

"That was great," Richardson said. "How'd you do that? Hypnosis?"

"That combined with his lust for women. My first success. Be happy. You're made of stronger stuff than him. Come on. Before we go, let's get whatever files your paper has on Thorne, his family, and Sullivan."

CHAPTER TWENTY

After dropping by the Los Angeles Herald, Frank drove everyone to the UCLA campus, where they all went to Mueller's office in the Anthropology Department. His secretary, Ida, passed him his messages, and he told her that the only person that could disturb them was Spade.

"Another message from the University of Arizona," Abraham said, "wanting us to move to Tucson and teach there."

"Arizona's nice most of the year," Tori offered, "and you don't get the humidity in the summer that you do here off the Pacific Coast."

"But Tucson is not exactly a thriving center for civilization."

"It's getting better, Abraham," Tori said. "Trust me."

Mueller smiled and looked over at Richardson. "Let's see what's in these files you brought over from the Herald."

Tori, Abraham, Richardson, and Frank all took turns looking

over each of the files on Sullivan and the Thorne Family. After about 15 minutes, Abraham looked around and commented, "I think most of the world would have a motive to kill Thorne. His company's reputation and personal acts are the walking definition of robber baron."

"Fortunately," Tori said, "most of the world was not at the museum last night."

"Well," Abraham said. "Who do we think is the best suspect now?"

"I would say Sullivan is the worst one," Richardson replied. "He owes everything to Thorne."

"Then again," Tori said, "the villain is sometimes the one you least suspect. There could have been a power struggle between the two reactionary zealots."

"Maybe," Abraham said. "The two children still had the most to gain, especially if one or both had an inkling the father was going to cut them off."

"The son also hated the father for driving away the woman he loved," Frank said.

"Good point, Frank," Tori said. "Do the files have anything on her?"

"Amazingly not," Richardson replied. "Somehow, they kept the affair out of the gossip columns. We don't know anything about her."

"If love is a motive, then Grantham has one too," Abraham said. "He's in love with Agatha and detested Thorne. That could be a powerful combination."

"Maybe," Spade said, beaming as he walked into the office. "But my vote is still on Sullivan."

"Why is that, Julian?" Abraham asked.

Spade took out a piece of paper and placed it on Abraham's desk. It was a flyer to the Sullivan rally that evening at the Hollywood Bowl.

"Guess where the men I followed dropped off the mummy and the other crate?"

"That kind of tips the scales one way, doesn't it?" Tori said.

"It would seem so," Abraham said.

"Should we tell the Police Chief and let him know we've found the Mummy?" Richardson asked.

"I'll see to that," Abraham replied, getting up and opening a cabinet behind him. He pulled out a bottle of scotch and some glasses.

"Isn't it a little early?" Spade said.

"Not in the least for what we're up against," Abraham replied. "Richardson, do you want some?"

"Sure."

"How about you, Julian?" Abraham asked, pouring the liquor into two glasses.

"Maybe later, Abraham."

"Suit yourself, I know Tori and Frank won't take any. I guess it's just us, Richardson."

Abraham handed a glass to Richardson, who downed the whole drink before Abraham even touched his.

"That's good stuff," Richardson said, immediately feeling the drowsing effects. He started to bend his head toward the desk. "Damn good stuff."

Tori helped set Richardson's head comfortably on the table.

"Don't want him hurting himself," Tori said.

"That's a switch," Abraham replied.

"Powerful scotch," Spade said.

"He'll be out for hours," Abraham said, "and out of harm's way like the police we aren't going to call. Any objections?"

No one said anything.

"Frank," Abraham said. "Stay here and keep an eye on Richardson."

"But Master," Frank said. "I will be of more use helping you and the Mistress."

Abraham thought for a moment. "Stay here for now. If we're not back by 10:00 p.m., come look for us."

"Yes, Master."

"Alright then," Abraham said. "Let's get ready for tonight."

"Hopefully, after this evening, we'll all be free of our curses," Spade said.

"That would be nice," Abraham said.

"Nothing but our and the world's future riding on what we do," Tori said. "No pressure."

CHAPTER TWENTY-ONE

October 16, 1928
Bay Cities Italian Deli and Bakery
Santa Monica, California
About 4:00 p.m.

A gatha, Ava, and Trevor had lunch at the Bay Cities Italian Deli and Bakery. Thomas was invited, but he said he had some errands to run before he could join them.

"This is a new beginning for the family and us," Agatha said, holding both Ava and Trevor's hands.

"Think what your newfound wealth can do," Ava said. "In addition to bolstering women's rights, we could help advance causes for retirement pensions, free health care, a minimum wage, and a cure for polio here and across the country."

"That's very true," Agatha replied. "Would you like to be the head of the foundation Thomas and I are thinking of creating? It would promote causes that advance the public good."

Ava was flattered and awed. "You want me, a Latina, to head your foundation?"

"I can think of no one better," Agatha replied.

Tears fell from Ava's eyes. "I would be honored, my friend."

"Wonderful," Agatha said, clasping her hands. "This will be great."

"And what about you two?" Ava asked. "When is the big day for you two?"

"I don't know," Agatha replied, cuddling up to Trevor. "I'm waiting for someone to ask the question."

"On that note," Trevor said, pulling out a small box and opening it, showing off a one-karat ring.

Agatha became flushed with excitement.

"In front of your best friend: Agatha, I ask you to be my wife. I will love and take care of you as long as I have breath. Will you marry me?"

"Yes, Trevor, yes."

The happy couple hugged and kissed each other, and Trevor put the ring on Agatha's finger. She showed it off to Ava, sharing her happiness. "What do you think, my maid of honor?"

"I think it's lovely. I'm sure Thomas will, too."

"Where is he?" Grantham asked, looking around. "He should have been here by now."

"We'll tell him later," Agatha said. She leaned over and whispered into Trevor's ear, "Let's get back to the hotel and celebrate. Hopefully Thomas and Colin are still running errands."

When they exited the deli, Ava bade Agatha and Trevor congratulations again and goodbye.

Agatha and Grantham looked for a cab to take them back to the apartment. Before they could hail one, a police car drove up beside them. A tall, dark-haired man, dressed in a police officer's uniform, opened the passenger side door, and came out.

"Trevor Grantham, Agatha Thorne."

"Yes," Grantham replied.

"I'm Officer Felix Douglas. Chief Bridges asked me to bring you back to your hotel. He has some questions to ask you."

"He does?" Agatha frowned. "I thought the murderer had been caught."

"All I know is he asked me to bring you. Please come with us."

The couple looked at each other and seemed confused.

"Well," Grantham said, holding the door for Agatha, "let's get this sorted out."

Agatha and Trevor went into the back seat.

"At least we won't have to pay for cab fare," Agatha said.

"Thank you for your cooperation," Officer Douglas said, entering the front seat and signaling the driver to go.

Agatha turned to Trevor and held his hand.

"I know I've been saying this a lot since last night, but we can do a lot of good things now that my father is out of the picture."

"Every cloud has a silver lining, my dear," Grantham said.

"Were you able to talk to Spade about the six-month extension?"

"No, I dropped by his apartment before joining you ladies for lunch, but he wasn't there. I'll call him later."

Grantham looked out the window and frowned. "Excuse me, Officer Douglas. This isn't the route to the Normandie Hotel."

"Damn," the police officer muttered.

"What did you say?" Agatha asked.

"I said damn, Miss Thorne," Douglas replied, turning back to face them. "I didn't think you were that familiar with the geography of the Los Angeles area roadways."

"What the hell?" Grantham yelled. "PULL OVER!"

"I can't do that, sir," Officer Douglas said.

Grantham unbuckled his seat belt and leaned into the front seat, but the police officer pushed him back, took out a blow dart and stuck him with a tranquilizer, instantly knocking him out. He slumped in the space between the front and back seat.

"WHAT DID YOU DO TO HIM?" Agatha yelled, reaching over to find Grantham's face.

"He's just knocked out, Miss Thorne," Officer Douglas replied, sticking Agatha with another tranquilizer. She slumped backwards and fell asleep.

Felix looked at the driver.

"At least we've been spared their endless chatter for the rest of the trip."

"Yeah," the driver said. "They sounded annoying."

CHAPTER TWENTY-TWO

October 16, 1928
The Hollywood Bowl
About 7:00 p.m.

*T*his is like a MAGA rally, Tori thought as she, Abraham, and Spade walked around the edges of the crowd. They were holding signs that easily could have been at a White Nationalist, KKK, America First, Trump Rally. *I knew there were groups like this in this historical period,* she thought to herself, *but I did not fathom how popular they were until now.* She looked at Abraham. "Can I have my dinner now? The world won't miss these dregs of society."

"Control yourself," Abraham replied. "Over the millennia, Julian and I have seen worse reactionary movements than this one."

"True," Spade said. "Remember when they went after the Wiccans? And The Reign of Terror in France?"

"Those were both close calls for me."

At about 7:15 p.m., Sullivan walked out the center of the stage in his formal religious attire. His followers showered him with applause until he reached the podium and held up his hand.

"My friends and children. We are at a crossroads in our holy mission to protect this country from those who would change the order of society and replace us."

The crowd booed those who they thought were a threat to them and shouted, "They will not replace us. They will not replace us."

"That's right," Sullivan said. "The Jew will not replace us. The Catholic will not replace us. The Moslem will not replace us. The Black will not replace us. The Hispanic will not replace us. The Chinese and the Jap will not replace us. The Indian will not get his land back."

The crowd roared their approval again.

"Holy shit," Tori muttered.

"They know we are onto them, and they know we will never give up the crusade to eradicate them from our society. Last night, they struck at us by taking away our wise benefactor, Malcom Thorne."

The crowd booed and hissed.

"Don't believe the Jewish press when they say it was the mummy's vengeance that killed our hero. It was the dark forces that want to replace you and take this country away from us that killed him."

The crowd roared "NO!"

"Now is the time to plan," Sullivan said. "If the next person to win the White House, whether it is the socialist Mr. Hoover or the Pope's apostle, Mr. Smith, continues this drive to make this country a haven for the ungodly, then we must be ready to storm the Capitol and take this nation back before the new president takes power in March."

The crowd all roared their approval, yelling "YES!"

Tori, frightened at the implications of Sullivan's words, grabbed Abraham's shoulder. "What he's calling for never happened. We must stop this zealot before he does something that affects reality."

"What is she talking about, Abraham?" Spade asked.

"If it didn't happen," Abraham said, glancing warily at the crowd, "that must mean his movement didn't get that powerful."

"I think that's because we stopped him," Tori said. "Imagine what he could do with the Eye of Aten now that he has the words on the tablet. We have to act now, tonight. Otherwise, he will use the Eye and its powers to take over the country. I wish Frank was here. We could use him."

Abraham looked in Tori's eyes and felt that she was probably right. "Julian, where did you see those drivers take the mummy and the other crate?"

"Over there," he pointed. "Backstage."

"Okay, let's make our way over there."

Spade led the way to the backstage area. No one paid attention to the trio, as the rest of the crowd was captivated by Sullivan's ranting. As they came closer, they were intercepted by Felix and some henchmen. The all held revolvers.

Tori started her vampiric transformation, but Abraham waved her off. "Not now. There are too many people here."

"Reverend Sullivan welcomes you and would like you to attend a private ceremony backstage," Felix said.

The trio looked at each other.

"Of course," Abraham said. "Thank you. Lead the way."

With two of the henchmen in front and another one in the back, Felix led them to the backstage rooms. There, they saw Agatha and Grantham, both tied to chairs and gagged. Behind them were Thomas and Colin, standing up and looking upset.

"We're so sorry," Thomas said. "We didn't want this to happen this way. Lock them all in the other room until the Reverend is ready for them."

CHAPTER TWENTY-THREE

October 16, 1928
The Hollywood Bowl
Close to Midnight

What seemed like hours passed after Tori and the others heard the end of the rally, but they were still confined to the small storage room with only a lantern for light. They could hear the voices of Thomas, Colin, and Sullivan in the other, larger room but could not quite make out what they were saying. Tori was getting impatient with Abraham's order to not transform, pacing back and forth in the room. That activity started to annoy the two other immortals.

"Could you stop that?" Spade asked. "You're pacing more than an expectant father in the maternity wing."

"Sorry," Tori responded, giving Abraham an ugly stare. "We could have been out of here hours ago if you would let us use our skills."

"We have to wait for the right time," Abraham said. "You must be patient."

"I'm so sick of you acting like Yoda."

"Who?" Spade asked.

"Never mind."

The door opened, and Felix entered, holding his revolver. "The Reverend and the others are ready to see you now."

"Good," Abraham said, taking the lead and whispering to Tori, "Wait for it."

Felix led them to the larger room. Sullivan was beaming, fully energized, and confident after his rally performance. Thomas and Colin were standing by the still-tied and gagged Agatha and Grantham. They both appeared dejected and remorseful. The crates containing Sennefer and the mysterious cold contents were in the middle of the room.

"It's good to see you again," Sullivan said. "Where is your big friend—the Golem-photographer—and that reporter?"

None of the trio responded.

"Never mind," the Reverend said, waving his hand. "I have men searching the grounds. If they're here, we'll deal with them."

"So," Tori said, speaking up. "You killed your patron and friend just so you could use him as a martyr for your cause to take over the country next year."

"Actually, no," Sullivan said, shaking his head. "I did not want Malcom dead. We had great plans that we wanted to accomplish with the recovery of the Eye and the tablet. Unfortunately," he said, looking at Thomas and Colin, "we didn't realize there were others with different designs for the artifacts."

The trio looked at Thomas and Colin.

"I guess it *is* the butler that did it," Abraham said. "Why? Revenge? The thought of controlling Thorne Industries? World Domination?"

"BECAUSE," Thomas yelled, "that son of a bitch father of mine caused the death of the love of my life, my mother, and my brother."

"What are you talking about, Thomas?" Agatha mumbled through her gag. "What about mother and Gilbert?"

"We found out after Jessica died in Italy. When Colin and I went over to retrieve her body, we ran into a police investigator who father bought off after he found out that it was Cain, acting on father's orders, who sabotaged the brakes in mother's car."

"Why did your father want to kill them?" Abraham asked.

"So, he could get total control of mother's money. He made sure Gilbert was in the car, so he wouldn't be around to inherit when he came of age."

"Thorne had his wife and stepson killed for money," Tori said. "Why am I not surprised? But how does that connect with what happened to your girlfriend?"

"We found out that Cain, acting on father's orders, poisoned Jessica and made it look like a suicide."

"Your father was true scum," Tori said. "I don't blame you for wanting revenge."

"Revenge and a chance for happiness," Thomas said, walking to the other crate. "Come over here."

With Felix and the other men watching them, the trio joined Thomas and Colin at the open crate. They peered in and saw the body of a young woman. She was dead but had been frozen for some time.

"The woman you loved," Spade said.

"*Love*," Thomas shot back.

"My daughter, Jessica," Colin added.

"Daughter," Tori repeated.

"My wonderful child. That bastard Thorne didn't even remember her name. He didn't even have the decency to express his sympathies to me and say how sorry he was for what happened to my baby."

"But how?" Abraham asked. "What happened?"

"She went away to school to study fashion design and came

back several years later," Colin said.

"That's when we fell in love," Thomas said. "We were soul mates."

"So, you wanted the Eye for the chance to bring her back," Abraham said.

"After she died, we had her body frozen and shipped to us. We stored her in a freezer at the warehouse until the time was right. We approached Andoheb, and he carried out the tasks."

"Which included killing my butler and taking the tablet," Spade said.

"We're so sorry, Mr. Spade. I had Andoheb kill those men for exceeding their instructions. Your butler was not supposed to be hurt."

"And Cartwright?" Abraham asked.

"He would have been a problem with our plans for the company," Thomas said. "It was necessary."

"Why not just fire him?" Tori asked, thinking about Cartwright's eye lodged in the window sill.

"And risk messy and costly corporate litigation?" Thomas said. "This was simpler. Besides, he was just as bad as our father. He just did a better job of hiding behind his professional demeanor."

"Hold on a minute," Tori said. "If you brought Jessica here, why not your mother and brother? The tablet should work on them."

"My father had them cremated," Thomas said. "We can't do anything for them."

"So why are you aligned with this zealot-charlatan?" Tori asked, pointing to Sullivan.

"Not by choice, Miss," Colin replied.

"When I was talking to Cartwright, I saw them and the other man, the Arab, enter the room where Malcom was killed during the blackout at the museum," Sullivan said. "It wasn't hard to figure out what they had done."

"Why didn't Cartwright say he saw them?" Tori asked.

"His back was to them when they entered the room," Sullivan replied. "It wasn't hard to contact Thomas and Colin this morning and persuade them to cooperate with me after I had my men find the warehouse and take possession of the items."

"So," Tori said, "you'll coerce them to give you financial resources to back your crusade against Hoover."

"Or the Papist Smith, if he wins the Presidency."

"And after that?" Abraham asked.

"The possibilities are endless now that I have the Eye and the Tablet. I can establish a White Christian Empire in this country and perhaps around the world. But first, let's see if the Eye actually works. Take the gag off Grantham and bring him here."

Felix motioned one of his men to stand Grantham up and bring him over. After taking off his gag, Sullivan took hold of the Eye with one hand and grabbed the tablet with another. "Now, Grantham. Would you please read the hieroglyphics on this tablet for me?"

"You can't read it?" Abraham asked.

"No," Sullivan said, holding the tablet in front of Grantham.

"Go to Hell," Grantham said.

"Predictable," Sullivan said. "He needs an incentive. Felix, put your revolver to Miss Thorne's temple and blow her brains out."

Agatha screamed, and Thomas stood between her and Felix. "Don't do this, Sullivan!"

"I guess we may have to make do without the wealth of Thorne Industries," Sullivan said. "Shoot Mr. Thorne, Felix."

"NO!" Colin roared, jumping in front of Thomas, as Felix fired. The shot hit the butler's abdomen, and he fell to the floor.

"COLIN," Thomas screamed. He knelt by Colin, who was gasping for breath. "I'm so sorry, my old friend. Don't go. I meant it when I said earlier you were the one who was most like a father to me."

"And you were like a son to me," Colin, choking and coughing, replied. "Just bring my little girl back, Thomas." The butler's eyes closed, and Agatha and Thomas both cried.

"Relax, Mr. Thorne," Sullivan said. "If this works, he'll be up in a minute." The Reverend pushed the tablet under Grantham's chin. "Now read this unless you want your friends dead."

"Hold on," Spade said. "I can read those hieroglyphs."

"What the hell are you doing, Julian?" Abraham asked.

"Very well," Sullivan said, handing the tablet to Spade. "Any tricks, and all your friends except Grantham die."

"Tori," Abraham said, and they quickly transformed into their supernatural personas.

"A vampire and a werewolf," Sullivan said in awe. "Kill them!"

Tori and Abraham turned to Felix and his men. The frightened henchmen emptied their weapons, but they had no effect on the vampire and werewolf, who made quick work of tearing their throats out.

"Holy shit," Grantham said.

Outside the backstage rooms, Richardson and Frank could hear the commotion from the back of the amphitheater, including the werewolf growls. "I think I know where they are," Richardson said. "Follow me, Frank."

They walked down the aisle to get to the backstage area, but two of Sullivan's men came to intercept them. "We were expecting you two," one of the men said, taking out his pistol. "Follow us, and don't make trouble. Mr. Sullivan told us how to shut off your big Golem friend."

"I see," Richardson said, looking down. "Did he also tell you how to shut *this* off?" Richardson pulled out a small pistol of his own and fired, knocking the gun out of Sullivan's henchman's hand.

Frank descended on the distracted men and overpowered both of them.

"I think we make a good team, big guy."

"Amazing," Frank replied.

"Heh, you're funny, too." Richardson grabbed the lantern from the small room. "Let's go get the scoop of the century."

Done with the henchmen, Tori and Abraham turned their attention to Sullivan. "Time to face God, Reverend," Tori said. The two jumped to take down the zealot, but he moved backward and desperately held up the Eye of Aten, yelling "STOP!"

Tori and Abraham were paralyzed and reverted to their human forms.

"I guess the Eye gives the holder some powers without the tablet," Sullivan said, eyeing the gem. "Now read the tablet, Spade, or I'm about to find out if I can crush your friends where they stand."

As Spade started to read the tablet, the crates started moving, and Colin opened his eyes.

"Keep going," Sullivan demanded, tightening his grip on the Eye. Spade continued.

Colin's wound healed, he stood up, and hugged Thomas.

A moment later, Jessica emerged from her crate, looking around and setting her eyes on her lover first, then on her father. "Thomas, father. What is happening? What am I doing here?"

The men rushed to her and helped her out of the crate. Thomas kissed her, and Colin hugged her.

"Everything is going to be fine, my darling," Thomas said. "We're so glad to have you back."

"Back from what?" Jessica asked, trying to take in her surroundings. "Where am I?"

"We'll explain later," Colin said.

A hand emerged from the other crate, and a man pulled himself up. It was Sennefer, fully restored to what he looked like just before Spade killed him. In Egyptian, he asked, "Who has disturbed my eternal rest and brought me back from the other world?"

"I have, old friend," Spade replied in Egyptian.

"The heretic," Sennefer said, frowning. "What sort of garments are you wearing? Where am I?"

"It's a long story."

Sennefer's face twisted into a grin. "Do you seek release from my curse?"

"I do. I am ready to face Aten's justice in the next life. But you must also deal with the evil heretics that brought you back. They do not believe in the ways of Aten."

"I will," Sennefer replied. "But first, I will give you the freedom you seek." Sennefer walked over to Spade and picked him up with one hand.

"Thank you," Spade said, closing his eyes.

Sennefer smiled and crushed Spade's neck, squeezing the life out of him. After finishing with his old enemy, Sennefer dropped Spade's body to the floor, saying "vengeance is mine." He turned and saw the frozen Abraham. "I remember you. You were a warrior for the heretic." Sennefer walked toward Abraham to finish him off, but Sullivan stepped in front of him.

"Wait! You must obey me. They can be useful to us in our holy crusade."

Sennefer knocked Sullivan to the ground, speaking again in the Egyptian language the reverend did not understand. "You have no control over me, false prophet. You, too, must face Aten's wrath."

Sullivan was still holding up the Eye of Aten and commanding it to stop Sennefer.

"Fool," Sennefer said. "The eye alone cannot influence a priest of Aten."

Seenefer grabbed Sullivan's face and chillingly smiled at him. "Reverend Lee is waiting for you on the other side, False Prophet." Sullivan, his eyes widened with total fear, yelled "NO." Seenefer muffled his other cries for mercy and bashed his head against the wall, bashing his skull and killing him instantly. He then bent down and took the Eye of Aten from Sullivan's limp hand.

The death of the reverend freed Tori and Abraham from his hold on them.

"One problem down," Tori said, shaking out her legs, "another unforeseen one to deal with."

Tori and Abraham transformed back to their vampire and werewolf selves and charged the mummy.

"What are they?" Jessica asked Thomas.

"I think they're the good guys. Let's get Agatha and Grantham and get out of here."

Sennefer fought off Tori and Abraham with the power of the Eye, pushing them both away from him.

"Why can't we defeat him?" Tori asked.

"Because he's a priest of Aten, the Eye must be making him stronger," Abraham said. "Keep trying!"

Frank and Richardson, armed with his gun and the lamp, entered the room just as Thomas and Colin untied Agatha and Grantham.

"Holy shit" Richardson said, yet again. "The mummy really is alive. Frank, Go help your masters."

The Golem rushed over to tackle Sennefer, and he seemed to be up to the challenge, pushing the mummy across the room.

"Frank!" Tori yelled. "Get the Eye from him and destroy it."

"Tori, what about a cure for us?" Abraham said.

"We don't have that luxury right now. Frank, get the Eye."

Grantham went for the tablet. "I think I can stop him by reversing the wording on the tablet."

"Won't that hurt Jessica and Colin?" Thomas asked.

"No! I'll specify Sennefer in the command."

"Do it," Agatha said.

Tori and Abraham attempted to help Frank tackle Sennefer

again, but the mummy, fully energized, was able to push all of them away.

Grantham started to recite the prayer backward.

Sennefer realized what he was doing and tried to stop him. Frank grabbed him from behind and pulled Sennefer back, managing to take the Eye of Aten from his hand. The Golem crushed it, causing the mummy to yell in anger. As Grantham finished reversing the prayer, Sennefer started to return to his mummified form. Dying and furious, he charged anyone within reach.

Grantham dropped the tablet to the floor, breaking it into many fragments. He urged the others to step on the pieces, pulverizing them further. Sennefer, fully back in his mummified form, roared in anguish. Richardson threw the lantern at him. It hit him squarely in the chest and broke apart, dousing him in flames. A moment later, he was barely more than a pile of ash on the floor.

Tori and Abraham returned to their human forms and surveyed the carnage.

Mueller went to Spade's limp body and knelt beside him, touching his shoulder. "I hope you've found release, my friend."

Tori hugged Frank and Richardson. "We are so glad to see you two."

"We had to get past Sullivan's men," Richardson replied. "Frank was able to take care of them."

"The talkative one helped," Frank said, cracking a small smile.

"So, Sullivan and his people murdered Thorne and the others?" Richardson asked.

Tori and Abraham looked at the others and then at each other.

"That's it exactly," Tori said. "That's what we'll tell Bell and Bridges."

"But Spade," Richardson said, glancing at his body. "What will we say happened to him? How do we explain the mummy's remains on the floor?"

"In the grand scheme of things," Abraham said, "I think the police would prefer the simpler explanation of us overpowering Sullivan and his underlings rather than the tale of The Mummy's Vengeance."

"Are you kidding?" Richardson said. "This is the story of the century, and we still have 72 years to go!"

Abraham sighed. "Do you remember our discussion from earlier, William?"

"I do, but come on. Be reasonable here."

"Besides, where's your evidence?" Tori said, raising an eyebrow. "The Eye and the tablet have been destroyed, and there's not much left of Sennefer."

"What about the witnesses?" Richardson asked.

"Based on this evening's events," Abraham said, looking around the room. "I don't think they'll be willing to talk to the press or the authorities. Am I wrong there, people?"

"You're absolutely right, Professor Mueller," Colin replied, speaking for everyone in the Thorne entourage. "You can count on our silence."

"Hold on," Richardson said, staring at Jessica. "Who's this other girl?"

"My fiancé," Thomas said, putting his arm around her.

Richardson blanched. "The *dead* one?"

"Dead?" Jessica repeated. "But I was just in the cottage drinking a cup of coffee."

"I'll explain later, dearest," Thomas said, glaring at Richardson. "Keep your big mouth shut, Richardson, and we'll make it worth your while. Do we understand each other?"

Richardson looked around the room and realized he was facing a unified front. "I'm ruined."

"Not at all," Tori said. "You'll still get your scoop and report the murder in an exclusive. Hell, you could still call it 'The Mummy's

Vengeance' because it would be the perfect theme to describe how Sullivan and Thorne's greed and thirst for power was the real curse that did them both in. You just leave out the stuff that even your editor, based on your earlier reporting and lack of strong evidence, would be reluctant to publish."

"That could work," Richardson said, giving in.

"Our sentiments exactly," Abraham said. "Let's call the police. Richardson has a Pulitzer to win."

CHAPTER TWENTY-FOUR

November 4, 1928
Orpheum Theater
Los Angeles

I n the almost three weeks since the deaths of Thorne, the bodyguards, Cartwright, Spade, and Sullivan, Richardson received praise for his reporting of the events at the Hollywood Bowl. To make sure that he did not open his mouth about what really happened, the Thorne heirs saw to it that he was assigned as the lead reporter at City Hall with a substantial pay raise funded in part by a grant from the Thorne Foundation. They also contacted connections on the Pulitzer Committee to consider him for an award. In his first week on the job, Richardson scored a major scoop with the uncovering of a bribery scandal involving a councilman and organized crime. However, when he would get an urge to write anything about the events involving Sennefer and the Eye of Aten, Tori, Abraham, and Frank would take turns stopping by his office or apartment to see how he was and take him out to lunch.

The museum director, Sommers, who no longer had a mummy

exhibit or Eye to show viewers, was also taken care of with a donation for a new museum wing and the entirety of Malcom Thorne's art collection, which consisted of 40 priceless paintings and sculptures from all of history's eras.

After being discharged from the hospital and investigating the events at the Hollywood Bowl, Detective Carl Bell had many questions about how the mummy, Eye, and tablet were destroyed. Tori and Abraham said the mummy and artifacts were destroyed during the fight. Even though Bell wasn't entirely convinced, Chief Bridges, who just launched a campaign for the now-vacant city council seat made available by the Richardson exposé, saw to it that the case file was closed.

With Jessica back, Thomas bribed a recording clerk in Genoa, Italy to destroy her death certificate. From there, Agatha and Thomas thought it would be wise to move to one of their father's private islands in the Mediterranean and run Thorne Industries and the newly formed social justice and philanthropic foundation from there, at least for the transition period. Colin would be the financial empire's emissary to the outside world. Ava would head the foundation and travel the world, promoting causes and securing donations. While on the island, Agatha married Grantham and Thomas married Jessica.

Reverend Sullivan's organization fractured—several competing disciples tried to claim the White Christian Nationalist mantle of the dead zealot.

Everyone present that night attended Spade's funeral.

"I'm sorry you lost your friend, Bram," Tori said as the pallbearers lowered the casket.

"He got what he wanted," Abraham said. "Release. I'll miss him though. He became a good man."

"Like you," Tori said.

Abraham smiled.

In gratitude, the Thornes remembered to take care of their supernatural friends too, sending a check with all their names on it in the amount of $500,000.

Tori was still questioning whether they did the right thing when she, Abraham, and Frank attended the California premiere of *The Man who Laughs* starring Conrad Veidt at the Orpheum Theater.

"We are letting them get away with murder," she whispered.

"Like when you killed that rapist earlier this year?" Abraham said. "Malcom Thorne was scum, too. Thomas and Colin did the world a favor by getting rid of him. Who knows what he could have done with Sullivan."

"And Cartwright and Spade's butler?" Tori asked.

"Like Thomas said, Cartwright was no better than Thorne, and the butler was not supposed to be killed."

"I agree," a familiar voice said from the row of seats behind them.

They all turned and smiled. It was Josh from the Foundation.

"Josh," Tori said, reaching over to hug him. "How are you and the others?"

"We're all good. They say hi. How are you adjusting?"

"Getting easier every day," Tori replied. "Abraham and Frank have been a great help."

Josh shook both Abraham's and Frank's hands. "Thank you for taking care of our friend. We were worried about her."

"Our pleasure," Abraham replied, feeling the weight of the hammer and stake in his pocket.

"She's been very helpful to me to this last year, Master Josh," Frank said.

Josh was taken aback by the Golem's educational progress, thinking *I've stepped into The Bride of Frankenstein here.*

"So, what else brings you here, Josh, other than checking up on me?"

"I wanted to see how my inspiration for Conrad Veidt's face worked for the audience at the grand opening." He struck a pose and grinned.

They all laughed.

"Anything else?" Tori asked.

"The Foundation, especially the people at Grey Branch, want to thank you for taking care of Sullivan. If he'd lived, he would have been a temporal *nightmare*."

"Thank the mummy of Sennefer," Abraham said. "He sent that ass into the great beyond."

"Yeah, about that," Josh said. "I've also come with a tip for you three."

Tori started to feel uneasy, thinking that they were about to be recruited as contractors for the Foundation. "What's the tip?"

"It would be good for Mueller to take that job at the University of Arizona and start a separate detective agency in Tucson with the money the Thornes gave you."

"How did you know about the money?" Tori asked.

"Please," Josh replied, smiling. "Do you have to ask?'

"Why should we go?" Abraham asked.

"A lot of interesting adventures await you in Arizona."

"Oh God," Tori said, horror filling her eyes. "Are we part of another Jigsaw Case File?"

"No," Josh said. "God, no. This is part of the Case Files for the Nightfall Detective Agency."

"Nightfall Detective Agency," Abraham repeated. "Interesting name. Who runs that?"

"You will," Josh replied. "In about ten months from now in Tucson, Arizona."

CHAPTER TWENTY-FIVE

September 18, 1929
The Nightfall Detective Agency
1062 North Highland Avenue, Tucson Arizona

The trio surprisingly liked the more mellow atmosphere of Tucson. They were able to get a nice house and build several basement rooms underneath. Abraham was treated like a god by the Anthropology Department at the University of Arizona. While Mueller spent the first semester teaching and getting acclimated to the university community, Tori, Ida, and Frank spent time getting the offices ready for The Nightfall Detective Agency.

"I know I've said this a thousand times, but I really like that name," Ida said.

Tori smiled. "It captures what all three of us are about."

Mueller came in at about 3:00 p.m., and the trio gathered in his office.

"What do you think, Master Abraham?" Frank asked.

"I think this is going to be great. And Frank, please stop calling us Master and Mistress. You can call us by our first names."

"I don't think that would be appropriate, Master."

"Oy," Abraham said.

"We'll work on it," Tori offered.

Ida came into the office looking a little perplexed.

"What's wrong, Ida?" Tori asked. "We have no outstanding bills yet."

"I know, Miss Jacobsen," Ida replied. "I think we have our first client."

"That's wonderful," Abraham said. "Why do you look so concerned?"

"He looks… strange, sir," Ida replied. "I didn't even notice him come in. I looked up, and he was there, his head down. He asked to see all three of you."

"Bring him in," Tori said. "Frank, stand behind him during the meeting."

"Yes, Mistress Tori."

Ida opened the door and motioned for the man to come in. She was right. He looked disheveled and out of place. He kept his head down.

Abraham stood up, smiling, and offered his hand. "Good morning, Mr…?"

"Simon," the man replied, still bowing and not shaking Mueller's hand. "Ira Simon."

"Would you please sit down, Mr. Simon?" Frank said, sliding into place behind him.

"I'd rather stand, thank you."

All four members of the agency were a little concerned.

"How can we help you, Mr. Simon?" Tori asked.

"I need you to investigate The Utopia Institute."

"I remember hearing about that place," Tori said. "It came up in the Thorne murder investigation."

"Why do we need to investigate The Utopia Institute?"

Abraham asked.

For the first time, Simon lifted his head. There was a bullet hole through his left eye. "To find out who killed me."

We hope you enjoyed Case Files from the Nightfall Detective Agency: The Mummy's Vengeance.
We would like to hear your opinion, so please leave a review on Amazon.

To find out how Tori became a vampire and wound up in 1928 Los Angeles,please read
History's Forgotten: Part One

The Adventures of Tori, Abraham, and Frank will Continue in the Next Tale from the Case Files from the Nightfall Detective Agency:
THE TRAIL OF THE ZOMBIES
Coming Out around Halloween in 2024.

About the Author

David Gordon has been a social studies teacher, principal, and founding owner of the Grand Canyon College Preparatory Academy in Tempe, Arizona. He grew up reading and watching science and historical fiction. He is also a big baseball fan. David has combined his various passions in the Jigsaw series, which focuses on time-traveling teens thrust into major historical events—many of which never made the standard history books. He was born in New York and now lives in Arizona with the love of his life Gwyn. They are both dog people and enjoy travel and food—Italian, Asian, Middle Eastern, and Indian cuisines. Currently, he is also an Instructional Assistant at Roosevelt Elementary School in Mesa, Arizona and a blogger/journalist for Blog for Arizona.

**Please sign up for the Jigsaw Universe Newsletter at
www.davidalyngordon.com**

Made in the USA
Middletown, DE
05 November 2023

41862087R00086